JN324711

ラフカディオ・ハーンの英語クラス
Lafcadio Hearn's English Class

《黒板勝美のノートから》

平川祐弘［編］

弦書房

目　次

英文序文（English Foreword）……………………………………4

まえがき ………………………………………………………………6

ハーンの英語授業の特徴 ……………………………………………16

熊本五高生・黒板勝美のハーン授業ノート
　自筆原版・復元・日本語訳 …………………………………………23

新年に関する表現　29
感覚に関する言葉　31
会話における敬語　39
天皇、皇帝、紋章　45
光と影　47
仮定法　51
諺（1）　57
アルケスティスの物語　63
紙幣、硬貨　71
郵便　75
汽車　79
諺（2）　79
音（聴覚）　83
視覚　87
作文
　(1) Fun について　95
　(2) by と through の違い　97
軍、戦闘に関する語句　99
様々な動詞、名詞　105
否定疑問文　119
人称代名詞を目的語にとる心理動詞　125
　（charm、delight、amuse など）

Character（性格）　131
人の体格、外見を表す語句　137
家族、家庭　147
文学　153

内田周平の講義ノートについて……157

《解説》黒板勝美の生涯……159

「熊本時代のヘルン氏」黒板勝美……163

「五高に於けるヘルン先生」白壁傑次郎……168

English Foreword

The Gen Shobo Company, Fukuoka, having published *Lafcadio Hearn's Student Composition Corrections* in 2011 and *Lafcadio Hearn's English Lessons* in 2013, now publishes the third of the series: *Lafcadio Hearn's English Class*, which is comprised of the photographic reproduction, English transcription and Japanese translation of Kuroita Katsumi's notebook of Hearn's English class at Kumamoto Daigo Kōtō Chūgakkō, the so-called Kumamoto Government College.

Kuroita Katsumi (1874-1946) learnt English from Lafcadio Hearn (1850-1904) during the academic year 1892-1893. As is clear from this notebook, Hearn was a very tactful teacher of English. As an experienced writer he knew well the usage of English words, and explained their nuances very skillfully to his Japanese students.

Murakawa Kengo, one of Hearn's students at the same high school, writes as follows in the number 200 of the *Ryūnan*, the alumni bulletin, in 1925: "When teaching English grammar, Hearn never used a textbook; he did not dictate his lessons. With a chalk he wrote on the blackboard grammatical matters, which students copied silently. Teacher Hearn wrote them very smoothly." Hearn then went on to explain, by giving many examples. "When we read again our notebooks after school, we were amazed at the clarity of his exposition: Hearn's grammatical explanations were generally what was most needed to us Japanese students. His teaching ability was really wonderful."

Kuroita Katsumi recollected as follows in his article, "Mr Hearn's Kumamoto Days," which appeared in the 1904 November issue of the monthly *Teikoku Bungaku*, special number in memoriam Koizumi Yakumo: "Compared with other foreign teachers, whose lectures were very difficult to follow, Hearn's lecture was very clear, and it was natural that he was welcomed by us all.....When teaching English literature, Hearn first wrote the main points on the blackboard, and then explained them in detail in his own words. It was therefore very easy for us to write down his lectures. Hearn always spoke in simple words and phrases which were quite understandable. The vocabulary he used was not above the level of the Third or the Fourth National Readers. We enormously enjoyed Hearn's lessons."

Hearn himself wrote about his teaching experiences in his Kumamoto days in essays such as 'With Kyūshū Students' and 'Of the Eternal Feminine,' collected in *Out of the East* (1895). An interesting common topic is found both in Kuroita's notebook and Hearn's essay. Hearn in fact seemed to teach repeatedly the same story of Admetus, first to Kuroita's class and then to Yasukochi's class the following year. Hearn was very curious to know the Japanese young men's reactions to the Greek story of King Admetus. Admetus, knowing that he was doomed to die, was extremely afraid of death.

When the gods granted him life if someone should take his place, he asked his ninety-nine years old father to die for his son. The old man became angry and said, "You are not a true man. You are a beast." His wife Alkestis, however, willingly gave her life for her husband Admetus.

Hearn apparently was interested in differences in ethical attitudes of the Westerners and the Japanese deriving from respective cultural backgrounds. He quotes the name of Alkestis in his last work, *Japan, an Attempt at Interpretation*. Hearn thinks that the Japanese woman might be compared to the Greek type of noble woman. How to evaluate the Confucian cardinal virtue of filial piety in a modernizing society is a very interesting topic for comparative ethics. In Kuroita's notebook Hearn contrasted, for example, the position held by mothers-in-law in the West with that held in Japan and said almost sardonically that "the very word "mother-in-law" is a term for laughter in the West." As Hearn idealized traditional values in Japan, he sometimes harshly criticized Western customs. Kuroita's notebook shows not only Hearn's ability as a language teacher but also his willingness to become a Japan interpreter. This notebook also provides a precious look into Hearn's mind at work.

I should add some words about what became of the student Kuroita Katsumi afterward. From the Kumamoto Daigo Kōtō Chūgakkō he went to the Tokyo Imperial University, and studied in the Japanese History Department. He later became one of the most influential professors in the discipline of historiographical studies. It is worth noting that Kuroita's lifelong assistant was Minari Shigeyuki (1874-1962), who was also Hearn's most helpful assistant in his Tokyo days. Kuroita was also known among foreign Esperantists, as he was the first president of the Esperanto Society in Japan. The dean of Japanese historiography was a nationalist who had an internationalist view.

It seems that Kuroita gave his notebook to Professor Ichikawa Sanki, Director of the English Department, when the younger colleague of the Faculty of Letters began to collect materials concerning Lafcadio Hearn in the 1930s.

I thank Matsui Kumi, Kitano Itsuko, Nomura Kayoko, Makino Michiko, Makino Yoko and Makino Miki for their help in transcription and translation, Sekita Kaoru for generous financial donation, and Ono Shizuo of the Gen Shobo Company. Without their respect for Hearn, this publication was not possible.

Sukehiro HIRAKAWA, Professor Emeritus, Tokyo University

まえがき

平川祐弘

ハーンの種々の英語授業ノート

　今回ここに覆刻したノートは、後に大正・昭和前期の日本の国史学界の大御所となる黒板勝美（一八七四年九月三日生－一九四六年十二月二十一日歿）が熊本第五高等中学校生徒としてラフカディオ・ハーン（一八五〇年六月二十七日生－一九〇四年九月二十六日歿）の英語授業を筆記したものである。なお、ハーンの英語教育についてはすでに次のような記録が書物の形で活字化されている。

　明治二十三年四月四日に満三十九歳で来日したハーンはその年の九月から二十四年十一月にかけて松江の島根県尋常中学校で教えた。どのような授業をしたかは『知られぬ日本の面影』に収められた『英語教師の日記から』にハーン自身の手で活写されているが、そのほかに当時中学四年生で満十五歳の大谷正信（一八七五－一九三三）と五年生の田辺勝太郎（一八七二－一九三一）の英作文を添削したものが『ラフカディオ・ハーンの英作文教育』として二〇一一年に福岡の弦書房から西川盛雄、アラン・ローゼン教授監修で茶色のカバーで出版された。これを読むとハーンがいかに懇切丁寧に英語を教えたか、また日本の中学生に Ghosts とか What is the most awful thing などの課題で英作文を書かせることで日本の子供の考え方を探ったかがよくわかる。なおそのほかにも、当時中学二年生で満十四歳の落合貞三郎（一八七五－一九四五）がノートにコピーしたハーンが語った英語の物語が八つ、關田かをる氏の手で平川祐弘編『世界の中のラフカディオ・ハーン』（河出書房新社、一九九四）に覆刻されている。落合は松江中学校が昭和十五年に出した『座談会　旧師小泉八雲先生を語る』の中で中学二年の英語授業を回顧して次のように述べている。

　「ヘルン先生の授業は読方と書取と作文の三課目（を各二時間）、……書取の場合は、先生が読まれるものを順番に一人ずつ黒板へ出て書く。先生が直される。私達はそれを写す。それは耳で聴きとる力の養成にはよい練習であったと思う。」

　次に翌明治二十四年十一月からの熊本時代の教師生活については『東方より』に収められた『九州の学生たちと』にハーンの手で描かれているが、そのほかに明治二十六年から二十七年にかけて熊本第五高等中学校予科三級（旧制中学校第四学年相当）で満十七歳前後の友枝高彦（一八七六－一九五七）が習った系統的な英語の授業が、そのノートのコピーが北星堂の中土義敬関係の資料から見つかり、これは『ラフカディオ・ハーンの英語教育』として二〇一三年に同じく弦書房から平川祐弘監修で青色のカバーで出版された。それが公刊されるにいたる経緯は人の心を打つものがある。友枝が半世紀前に習ったハーンのノートを富山高校のヘルン文庫のガーディアンともいうべき高田力教授が借用して写し刊行

しようとしたのは一九四三年であった。しかし戦時下であるために北星堂は刊行できなかった。北星堂の中土義敬は平和回復の折には世に出そうと思い、高田ノートを念のため書き写したが、終戦前に亡くなった。友枝ノート、高田ノートは行方不明となったが、中土ノートが見つかったためについに日の目を見たのである。

　しかしこの友枝高彦・高田力・中土義敬ノートのほかにも熊本時代には黒板勝美（一八七四－一九四六）のノートがあった。黒板は、友枝より前に、おそらく明治二十五年から二十六年にかけて本科一級（旧制高等学校第三学年相当）、黒板が満十八歳の時と思われるが、ノートしたものが東大英文科の元市河三喜研究室に保存されていた。これは友枝ノートより四学年上級の英語授業であった（黒板は早く進級した生徒で、同級生は三歳ほど年長の者が多かった。その一人の赤星典太などは黒板の六歳年長、学年は一つ下の安河内麻吉も黒板の一歳年長であった）。

　Conversation 英会話という名目が第五高等学校当局がハーンに依頼した授業の一つで、その授業でハーンは英語の言葉のニュアンスを見事に説明している。このノートを読むと多くを教えられる。生徒が教えられるのは当然だが、日本人外国語教師の私どもが読んで実に多く教えられる。それでこの黒板ノートを覆刻し日本語訳も添え、これは『ラフカディオ・ハーンの英語クラス――黒板勝美のノートから』と題して二〇一四年同じく弦書房から今度は臙脂色のカバーで出版することとした。ちなみに卒業順にいうと黒板は明治二十六年熊本五高の第二回卒業生（明治二十九年の帝大卒業生）、友枝は明治三十一年の第七回卒業生（明治三十四年の帝大卒業生）、落合貞三郎は明治三十三年の第九回卒業生（明治三十六年の帝大卒業生）、仙台や京都の高校で学んだ大谷正信は明治三十二年の帝大卒業生ということになる。

　そのほかにハーンの英語授業の教材記録には、時代はそれより下る一八九八年以降、学習者の年齢も下がるが、長男一雄（一八九三－一九六五）に家庭で教えたものが『小泉八雲父子英語練習帳』として出ている。一九九〇年八月、松江の八雲会から銭本健二編で出たが、功を急いだためか不完全なものであり、翌年改訂版が出た。その前に出た Koizumi/Fellers, *Re-Echo* (Caxton, 一九五七) にもハーンが一雄に語った物語の数々が一雄のコピーブックから再現されているが、たいへん貴重な一冊となっている。

黒板ノートの覆刻

　前回の友枝ノートの出版に際しては富山高等学校（現富山大学）の初代校長でハーンの蔵書を富山に移管しヘルン文庫に保存した南日恒太郎の孫にあたる松井玖美氏から出版助成をいただいた。今回の黒板ノートの出版に際しては關田かをる氏から出版助成をいただいた。黒板ノートのトランスクリプションは富山八雲会の松井玖美、北野逸子、野村香代子、牧野美知子の四氏がまず目を通し、私を含めて七人がチェックした。その英文の日本語訳の作成及び欄外の註記には牧野陽子成城大学教授ととくに牧野美季成城学園高等学校

講師の助けをお借りした。実はこのノートを黒板のものと知らずにチェックした人が以前にもう一人いた。故銭本健二教授で、雑誌『ヘルン』29、30、31、32、34に『熊本第五高等中学校における英会話授業――ある学生の筆記ノートから（東京大学文学部英文科市河文庫所蔵）』という題で活字化を試みている。しかし『ヘルン』のトランスクリプションは何頁分もが脱落しており、杜撰(ずさん)で、はなはだよろしくない。学術出版と言える水準に今回の弦書房版で初めて到達したと私は考える。なお黒板ノートに見られるラフカディオ・ハーンの英語授業の特色については後掲の牧野美季論文が意を尽くしているので、その説明を見られたい。出版については今回も弦書房の小野静男氏以下を煩わした。

　そうした次第だから、關田氏が二〇一四年春、東大英文科研究室でご自分が「新発掘」したと言いたい気持はわからないではないが、二昔前に銭本教授が不完全な形ではあれ一度すでに世に出している以上、新発掘という言い方は大袈裟に過ぎると思い、その表現は取り下げていただくこととした。しかし關田氏の御芳志はまことに有難く、各位の協力のおかげでこんな立派な単行本が世に出た次第である。お礼申し上げる。

国史学界の大御所、黒板勝美

　ここでハーンの授業をノートした黒板について説明する。黒板は名前を勝美という。クロイタ・カツミと発音する。ノートの初めに、

　　この英文筆記ハ　余　熊本第五高等
　　中学にありし比　ラフカヂオ・ヘルン（小泉
　　八雲）氏の口授するところ　今にし
　　て　これを　読むも　猶　興味津々
　　たるを　覚ゆ
　　　　　大正十二年九月廿有一日夕
　　　　　　　　　　　勝美記

と書いてある。これを読めばたとえ姓は書かれていなくとも、ノートを書いた人が黒板勝美ということはわかってしかるべきではないだろうか。黒板勝美は日本の国史学界の大御所であった。

　このノートを読むと、旧制熊本高等学校の英語教育の水準の高さに驚かされる。黒板は一八九三年七月五高を卒業、帝大の国史学科に入学したが、そこでは六年前からドイツ人のルードヴィッヒ・リースが教えていた。日本の官学アカデミズムに文献的・考証的方法を教えた人と言われるが、その教育内容の実態は意外にはっきりしていない。ということは東大の歴史学が自分の足元をきちんと調べていない、ということでもある。たとえばランケ流の近代的な史学研究法を教えたというから、世間はすべてドイツ語で授業したと思

いがちだが、ケーベル先生の西洋哲学の授業同様、英語でも教えていたらしい。

　黒板が年齢の割に早く進級したということは彼が英才だったからであろう。英語がよくできる学生だった。すくなくとも日本史学者の中では断然よくできた。近ごろは英語を得意としないから国文・国史を選ぶ学生がいるといわれるが、黒板の場合はそうではない。ただし同じく九州出身でも肥後出身で十歳上の徳富蘇峰のような偉才に比べれば劣る。また黒板より一歳上だがエール大学で教えた朝河貫一とは比較にならない。

第四回世界エスペラント大会（ドレスデン）記念写真（明治四十一年八月）
（前列中央　ザメンホフ博士、左端　黒板）

　しかし黒板は日本史学者でありながら外国旅行が大好きであった。ただし英語で講演したとか英語論文を活字にしたとかいう形跡はない。それでも一度だけ外国でたいへん持てたことがある。一九〇八年八月ドレスデンで開かれた第四回世界エスペラント大会に出席した時で、大会の成功を報じた息子宛の葉書に「おとうさんはアッチからもコッチからも引張凧といふ有様で大持てにもてました」と本人が書いている。ザメンホフ博士を中央に十五人で記念写真を撮った際、三十代半ばの黒板博士は左端に座っている。立派な服装で押し出しも立派である。エスペラントまで手がまわったのはすでに英語もよくできたからであろう。

　黒板は一九〇二（明治三十五）年、満二十七歳で帝大講師を嘱託されている。ハーンが帝大を去るのは一九〇三年三月だからハーンとしばらくのあいだ同僚であったと言えないこともない。黒板はハーン没後間もない一九〇四年十二月に出た『帝国文学』「小泉八雲記念号」に『熊本時代のヘルン氏』という追憶記事を寄せ、「此ヘルン君の事を」と書き出している。ハーンは黒板より二十四歳も年長の外人教師である。よく「君」で呼べるものだ、と驚くが、黒板は熊本高等学校で先生生徒の誰しもが尊敬した秋月悌次郎のことも「先生」と呼ばず「君」と呼んでいる。慶応義塾では先生は福沢先生だけであとは「君」づけだというが、黒板はそうした慣行をよしとしたのかもしれない。しかし自身は黒板先生と周囲から奉られ、国史科や史料編纂所のボスであった。田口鼎軒を尊敬し『国史大系』を編纂した。主著は一九〇八年、三十四歳のときに出した『国史の研究』で「研究入門書としてゆるぎない地位を確保し続けた」と『20世紀の歴史家たち』（刀水書房、一九九九）に石井進が書いている。石井は彼自身が昭和後期の東大の日本中世史の教授だが、黒板を「忠君愛国の士、そしてエスペランティスト」というところが面白い、と評している。黒板の門下生で最初に東京帝大助教授になったのが平泉澄で、平泉は一代の大秀才だが、

戦後は皇国史観の主唱者としてさんざ叩かれた。ではその平泉をいちはやく助教授に登用した黒板が皇国史観の開祖かというとそういうことはない。黒板は『国体新論』（一九二五）でも「これまでの国体論がどうかすれば偏狭な独断的の議論に傾いて居り、小愛国に堕して誰人にも首肯せしむるやうなものの少ないことは如何にも遺憾である」と述べている。石井はその点に注意している。ハーンなどと同じで、黒板も国民的自負心をもち自国の精華の保存をはかるが、外国の特長で採るべきものは採る、という世界に向って開かれた愛国者であった。石井進は左がかっていたが皮肉な男で「言葉においてきわめて反体制的、行動において実は保守的体制的という方（戦後の口先左翼の日本史学者）とのおつき合いを重ねているうちに、いつしか逆に黒板に対する興味がつのってきた」と黒板紹介の一文の「おいがき」に書いている。

黒板勝美と三成重敬と梅謙次郎とハーン

　黒板を直接知っている日本史関係者の証言として興味深いのは『日本歴史』第百三十四号百三十五号（一九五九）に掲載された座談会『黒板勝美博士を偲びながら』であろう。三成重敬（みなりしげゆき）、高柳光寿、桃裕行、吉川圭三が話しているが一番話しているのは一番関係の深い三成重敬（一八七四─一九六二）である。三成の名はハーンに関心のある人には親しいであろう。ハーンの日本研究に貴重な資料を探してきて提供した一人は三成で、小泉節子が口授した『思ひ出の記』を文章化したのも三成である。

　三成は明治三十一年、東大の史料編纂掛写字生となり、三十六年から黒板の下で各地の古文書調査に当った。その年に黒板の学位論文『古文書様式論』を隅田川沿いの一流の料理屋で十日ほど清書した由である。黒板が書いたものを三成に「読んでくれ」といい、読んでわかればよしわからなければまた書き直す。そして後には黒板がしゃべって三成に美濃紙に博士論文を書かせたらしい。といっても大体原稿は出来ていてそれを清書するときにいろいろ訂正したとのことである。大村出身の黒板と松江出身の三成は同じ明治七年生まれだが、二人とも奇しくも同じ外人の先生に学んだ。三成は松江中学でハーンから英語を習ったが病身で吃音で当てられても声が出ず退学した。黒板は熊本高校でハーンについて学んだが英語もよくできた。同じ一八七四年生まれでも、帝大出身で自信も実力もあった黒板とそれなりに国学漢学国史の実力のあった三成であったが、身分的にこんな差をつけられてしまった。しかしその二人が親分子分で組んで仕事をしたところが面白い。

　三成重敬は松江藩士族の子で三歳のとき両親が死に母方の祖父玉木秀平の家で育てられた。秀平の長女の娘婿で商法・民法の権威梅謙次郎（一八六〇─一九一〇）の紹介で史料編纂掛に日給二十五銭で勤めた。三成は生涯独身であった。昭和三十七年二月、三成の葬儀の日にハーンの三男清はみずから生命を絶った。野獣派の画家として名を成していたが、清を蔭で支えてくれたのは三成だったからで、妻にも先立たれていたからである。三成重敬の母は玉木秀平の三女であった。秀平の長男の玉木十之助は小泉セツの実母チエの兄の

塩見小兵衛の娘を妻とし、あいだに玉木光繁・光栄ほかがいた。だから三成重敬は梅謙次郎、玉木光繁・光栄の従兄弟である。玉木光栄（一八八六－一九七一）は明治三十二年から三十七年まで五年間小泉家の書生であった。ハーンの『草ひばり』などの作品にもアキは実名で登場する。またフランス語が流暢な梅とハーンは親しく、心臓発作を起こした時も梅あてにフランス語で遺言をしたためている。梅はハーンの葬儀の委員長をつとめた。

　ハーンは梅から、日本の歴史や故事などに関する資料蒐集にもっとも適当な助手として三成を紹介された。書生の光栄の仲立ちで三成がハーンの牛込の家を訪ねた。そのときの様子を三成の話をもとに後藤昂（のぼる）が伝えている。「座敷で待っていると、八雲が静かに入って来て、会釈をして、座ると三成に対して、直ぐ片手で眼鏡のつるをつまんで、のぞき込むように、じーっと、暫く見つめていたが、「よき眼です。日本の侍の眼をしている」と褒めたという（『ヘルン』、19、20、21の後藤昂記事参照）。黒板でなく梅が三成をハーンに紹介したのである。なお本郷キャンパスで黒板がハーンに話しかけた様子はなく、その当時の思い出は述べていない。当時のハーンは日本人とも外人ともつきあわなかったといわれる。しかし梅謙次郎とはときどきフランス語で話していた。

　生徒に映じた熊本時代のハーン
　黒板の名前は熊本時代のハーンが五高の生徒のことを書いた『九州の学生たちと』にも、またチェンバレン宛の手紙にも出てこない。しかしそこに名前の出た日本人生徒がハーンの思い出を詳しく書いているか、というとそうでもない。日本人生徒の側では後に東大の西洋史学教授となる村川堅固（一八七五－一九四六）は黒板勝美より学年は二年下の生徒だが、ハーンの授業風景を後年次のように回顧している。

　　先生の教授法は一種独特のものであつた。例へば文法を教へらるゝにも教科書を用ひらるゝでなし、又口授筆記をさるゝでなし、……黒板に向ひ、チョークを取つて、左の上の隅から文法を書き始められる。生徒は黙々としてそれを写す。其の書かるゝのは些の渋滞なく、時間の終りの鐘のなるまで続く。鐘が鳴ると一礼して退出さるゝ。かくして写し来つた筆記帳を放課後読んで見ると、秩序整然、而も日本学生に取つて最も適切な文法上の注意が与へられて居る。先生は一片の原稿もなく、全時間些かの淀みなく書き続けられ、然もそれが極めて整つたものであつたのは驚くべき技倆と思ふ。これは先生の天稟の文才もあつたらうが、教場に出らるゝまでには、頭の中で十分練つて来られた事と思ふ。
　　その後英文学史を教はつた時も、全然此流儀でやられた。然も英文学史は文法の場合よりも、一層先生の文才を発揮せられたことは、勿論である。
　　　　　（村川堅固『母校に於ける小泉八雲先生』、『龍南』二百号、大正十五年十二月所収）

これは今回の黒板勝美ノートの内容をそのまま説明しているといえよう。
　『五高に於けるヘルン先生』について『龍南』二百号に回想を寄せている人にはほかに黒板より学年は一つ下の白壁傑次郎がいる。後に五高の教授になった人である。参考にこれも後ろに掲げるが、しかしかつての五高生の中でハーンの英語や英文学の授業の長所を一番見事に指摘しているのは黒板その人であろう。黒板の『熊本時代のヘルン氏』がそれで、これも全文後ろに掲げる。
　その中で「今まで居られた外国教師の非常に難解な聞き悪いレクチュアに比して我々は非常に好意を以て迎へた」と黒板は書いている。ハーンは英語とともに英文学も講義したが、それについては「其時分は黒板に大体を書きまして、其後で又詳しく自分で話をするといふ訳であつた。ですから筆記する方は楽であつた。それで能く分る言葉ですから殆ど分らないといふことは義理にも言へない訳であつた、それだから皆喜んで居つた。実に易(わかりやす)い言葉で、詰り程度で言つたら第三リーダーか第四リーダー位の言葉であつた」。
　黒板は教室以外でもハーンとつきあいがあった。松江でハーンから習った小豆沢八三郎が養子として入籍することになっていた藤崎家と黒板とは同じ大村の出の関係で懇意だったからである。八三郎が母方の親戚筋にあたる小泉家へ預けられていた関係もあり、小泉家によく遊びに行きハーンの話を聞いた。熊本も暖い所で蚊が多いがルイヂニヤの蚊は此処のよりも余程大きいなどという話も聞いたという（Louisianaを記憶違いでルイヂニヤと書いたので正しくはルイジアナである）。

ハーンの側の印象

　ハーンが五高生から受けた印象は『九州の学生たちと』に出ており、講談社学術文庫版小泉八雲名作選集『光は東方より』に収められている。黒板も回想の中でふれているがハーンは生徒に英作文をよく書かせた。熊本では What do men remember longest?「人はなにをいちばん永く記憶するか」とか「文学における永遠とは何か」とか「学校の第一日」とか『クオレ』の巻頭の章にヒントを得た出題をしている。英文学の話もした。
　黒板ノートとの関係で注目すべきはアルケスティスの話が『九州の学生たちと』にも黒板ノートにも出て来ることである。黒板ノートには話の筋が出ているが、古代ギリシャのアドメトス王が重病になり、身代わりになるものがいなければ王はこのまま死ぬという神託が下された。王は誰か自分のために命を差し出す者はいないか、とお触れを出したが誰も申し出ない。王の父は九十九歳になっている。アドメトスは父に「あなたはこれだけ長生きして人生を楽しんだのだから私の身代わりに死んでくださいませんか」と頼んだが、父は激怒する。すると妻のアルケスティスが「わたしがあなたの身代わりになって死にますから子供をよろしく頼みます」と言って死んだ。父は「お前が臆病者の畜生だと言ったのは本当だった。女ですらお前より勇敢だ。お前は自分の子供の母親を奪った人殺しだ」と非難して、親子は決別する。ハーンはこの話を五高生に聞かせて亀川徳太郎、安河内麻

吉、川渕楠茂、隈本繁吉らの感想を作品中に伝えている。日本人がこの種の状況に追い込まれた時にどのような判断を下すか、という興味深い比較倫理的考察といえよう。ギリシャ神話には極限状況とでも呼ぶべきシチュエーションが含まれる。もともと人間に思考実験を促す知的ゲームの要素が内在しているのだが、ハーンはアルケスティスの話を五高第二回卒業の黒板の学年にもその次の第三回卒業の学年にもした。安河内がいたのは第三回で、主としてそのクラスの生徒の感想をハーンは『九州の学生たちと』の第四節に引いている。長い感想を述べた生徒の作文は、ハーンが英文は手直ししてあるが、名前通りの本人のものだろう。その前後に出て来る生徒は、もしかすると名前は借りただけかもしれない。クラスがはるか下の友枝はともかく、ハーンがあげた名前の中に黒板がはいっていないのはどうしてだろうか。黒板は安河内ほど印象的な生徒ではなかったということか。

　なおハーンは遺著『日本——一つの解明』の Feudal Integration「封建の完成」の章の結びで日本の女性を論じ、一家の嫁として、妻として、母として、三重の役割をきちんと果たす日本の女はギリシャ・タイプの高貴な女性、アルケスティスにも比せらるべきものではあるまいか、と述べている。熊本時代から十年近く経って『日本——一つの解明』を書きあげた際も、このような評価を変えていないことは驚くに足ることである。黒板ノートを読むと、英語の授業の様子もわかって面白いが、日本研究者ハーンの頭脳の働きも垣間見えて来て興味ふかい。ハーンは日本の伝統的な価値観を高く尊重した。時には理想化した。そのハーンは日本との対比で西洋における mother-in-law「姑（しゅうとめ）」の位置に言及し、mother-in-law という言葉は嘲笑を誘うことさえあるのだ、と説明している。その実例が甚だしく手厳しい。

　ハーンは英語授業でも常に一石二鳥を狙う多力者であった。本人も英語を教えつつ日本人生徒から日本人の気持を探ろうとしていた。そして日本人の生徒もハーンから英語を学ぶことによって、英文学の趣味を覚え始めたのであろう。

黒板勝美と市河三喜

　最後に、ハーンと黒板勝美と市河三喜の関係にふれたい。
　關田かをる氏はこの黒板ノートの冒頭に墨書された「大正十二年九月廿有一日夕」と表紙裏に書かれた文字の最後に「一読スベキモノナリ　I. 生」と市河三喜のイニシアルが署名されているところから、これは大正十二年九月ころ、黒板教授がハーン資料の収集を呼びかけていた市河教授の要請に応じて渡したものだろうと推理した。そうかもしれないが、違うかもしれない。同じ書物に二種類の見方を異にする解説があるのも面白かろうと思い、筆跡鑑定と時代考証の見地から平川私見も書き加えさせていただく。
　赤インクで記された「一読スベキモノナリ　I. 生」の筆跡は黒板とは別人である以上確かに市河の意見であるように思われる。しかしその前の「Idiom ニ二種アリ……用井ルコト勿レ　用井ル時ハ……」の文章は、これとそっくりの筆跡の「用井ル」が黒板ノートの

中にもある以上、黒板の筆跡と見るべきだろう。また Sponteneity と誤って書いたのが英文科の主任の市河とは思えない。それからさらに問題なのはイニシャルの署名ははたして「I. 生」と読むべきだろうか。「T. 生」と読むべきではないだろうか。もし後者だとすれば一体誰だろうか。しかし誰であるにせよ、このノートが一読すべきものという感想に変わりはないのである。

　次にかりに「I. 生」が正しいとして、大正十二年九月に黒板がこのノートを市河に渡したか。その年は九月一日に関東大震災が発生し東京帝国大学の図書館は炎上した。そんな収拾のつかぬ事態の最中にハーン資料収集などが行なわれたはずはない。黒板がその時期にこのノートを市河に渡したとは考えられない。

　黒板家の長男であった勝美の熊本時代のノートが保存されていたのは長崎県東彼杵郡の実家だったのではあるまいか。東京の大学に合格し上京する際に高校時代のノートを持参する人はまずいないだろう。関東大震災の後、被災した人も被災しなかった人も多くが東京から地方に帰った。黒板もその一人だったのであろう。故郷の家に戻り、昔の講義ノートを見つけて読み返し「今にしてこれを読むも猶興味津々たるを覚」えたのではないだろうか。

　他方、市河三喜夫妻がハーンの資料収集を本格的に始めたのは、夫妻が一九三一（昭和六）年にカーン財団の基金で世界一周をしてからのことである。積極的にイニシアティヴをとったのは晴子夫人だった。夫妻が松江を訪ねたのは帰国の翌昭和七年である。市河夫妻が記念館設立を呼びかけ、それで一九三三（昭和八）年、松江に小泉八雲記念館は開設された。市河は本郷の英文科でもハーン関係の資料の収集を始めた。黒板は市河より十二歳年長の教授で、一九三五（昭和十）年、東大を定年退官する。市河教授が小泉八雲記念館の設立やハーン関係資料の収集に特に熱心だったのは市河が四十代後半のことで、黒板が文学部の年下の同僚の市河教授にノートを渡したのは、その昭和七年ごろから、遅くとも昭和十年、黒板が東大を去る前までの間、と考えてよくはないだろうか。

　二十世紀を通してハーン評価の浮き沈みはまことに激しかった。高橋節雄（一八七八－一九七一）は松江中学でハーンから習い、海軍兵学校を卒業、日本海海戦にも参加した。一九〇七年、日本製の巡洋艦筑波で世界一周したが、各地で高橋はハーンの直弟子ゆえに珍重され「全く先生の余韻に尾して世界を歩いた様なものであった」。西洋で日本人を見かけると話しかけてきた人にはハーンの読者が多かった。そのことは一九三一年の市河夫妻の世界一周のときまでなお続いた。しかし国際社会における日本の評価の低下に比例してハーンの評価も米英では低下した。一九四四年、米国で軍用船に「ラフカディオ・ハーン号」と命名しようとしたとき非難の大合唱が起こり米国海軍省は愛国者の名前に改名すると声明したほどである。日本の外国研究者は本国での評価を気にする人たちである。秀才や才媛であればあるほど米英の動向に敏感となる。戦後の東大英文科では中野好夫教授が一九四六年九月号の『展望』に小泉八雲を論じていちはやくけなした。そのせいでもあ

るまいが、東大にはハーン関係資料が多く保存されているにもかかわらず、きちんとしたハーン研究者は出てこない。「トウダイモト暗シ」とはまさにこのことであろう。一人の作家について日本側と西洋側でかくも好悪が分かれるのはなぜか。その評価の食い違いこそ比較研究の好対象となるのではあるまいか。

　戦中戦後の日本の英語教育界にはハーンから直接習った人々の影響力がまだ強く残っていた。ハーンの On Reading など実にすばらしい読書論であったが、一九四七年、中学四年の英語教科書に載っていた。私はそのころ福原麟太郎編の教科書で東京高師出身の、おそらく福原門下の中山常雄先生から *Kwaidan* を習った。その教科書の冒頭には外国を扱う英米作家についてその外国の土地の人がなんと評しているかも大切な目安だという趣旨の Drinkwater のハーン評が引かれていたかに記憶する。ハーンは日本の土地の人に愛された作家である。その福原氏の『近代の英文学』（研究社、大正十五年）に収められた『ラフカディオ・ハアン』の一文は一九二三年に書かれたものだが「あゝ初めて Lafcadio Hearn を読んだ時、私はどんなに親しい西洋人を彼のうちに発見した事であつたらう」に始まる。そんな好文章も市河教授は東大英文科のハーン・コレクションの中に取り揃えてあった。

　その私は東京高師付属中学から一九四八年に駒場へ進学した。そのころに耳にした過去の東京帝大名物教授列伝の中にこんなのがあった。定年退官する黒板のために知友門弟が集い謝恩会が開かれた。その宴の途中、黒板は起立して謝辞を述べ、これから資料調査に出かける、夜行列車の出発時間はしかじかなのでこれにて失礼する、と三成とともに会場を後にした、という。黒板勝美は学内のみならず学外でも文化財の保護のために多くの活動をした行動家でもあった。その黒板の面目を伝えるエピソードであるかと思う。その黒板は一九四六年に亡くなった。

ハーンの英語授業の特徴

牧野美季

　ラフカディオ・ハーンが熊本の第五高等学校の学生を対象に行ったこの英語授業では、外国人英語教師ならではの指導が効果的になされていること、また提示される素材や例文にハーンの文学者としての資質や関心が現れていることが、興味深い特徴としてあげられる。明治時代の地方都市で、教科書を使わずに、手作りで行われたものだが、現代の我々にとっても学ぶべき点は少なくない。

　まず、授業全体を通して、ハーンが最も力を入れたのは、語彙を導入する際に、母国語話者が無意識に使い分けている微妙なニュアンスや語源などの背景知識を説明することだったことがわかる。学生にとって辞書の説明だけではイメージが摑みにくい、似たような意味を持つ語について、そのニュアンスの違いや、前置詞の有無による違い、複数形の有無などを、具体的かつ巧みな例文で、また時には図解入りで、細かく説明している。

　例えば、授業の冒頭は、年始の挨拶に関する表現から始まるのだが、そこで新年に関する話題として学生たちも新年に楽しむ花札の例が出される。そこでハーンは several と different という二つの語を取り上げる。辞書では前者は「いくつかの」、後者は「さまざまな」という語が与えられている二つの単語であるが、ここで several の場合は同じ種類のものの数を示し、different の場合には異なる種類のものの数を示す時に使われることを説明している。似たような複数の数を表わす語であっても、その違いに学生の注意を促すのである。また climb「のぼる」という語の説明では、そこに直接目的語が続く場合と、"climb on" というように前置詞が後に続く場合の違いを説明している。実際にどのような語が climb の直接目的語となり、反対に "climb on" と on が続く場合にはどのような語が使われるのかを具体的に示しながら、"climb on" には「到達すべき水平な面」が想定されているのだと指摘するところが、学生の理解を深めるという点で非常に有効だと言える。

　人間の五感に関する語彙の説明には、かなり時間をかけている。聴覚に鋭敏だったハーンらしく、「音」の形容詞を説明する際にも微妙なニュアンスの違いを示している。音を形容する語には loud「大きい」、low「低い」などの語のほかに、小さい音を表わす際に用いられる weak「弱い」、faint「かすかな」があることに触れ、さらに、特別な音を表わす形容詞として、力強く低い音を表わす deep、甲高く鋭い音を表わす shrill、甘美で心地よい音を表わす sweet なども同時に説明する。それらの音に対して、具体的にどのような音が相当するのかを、学生たちが想像しやすい例を多く取り上げ解説している。特

に sweet の説明に際しては、その語が「音」だけではなく「味」や「匂い」「性格」「顔つき」という多岐にわたる用法があることに言及し、その言葉の厚みを説いている。

また、同じ語に二つの意味が与えられているものの例として、ハーンは taste を取り上げる。taste には、肉体に関する感覚を表わし「味覚」を意味する場合と、精神に関する感覚を表わし「審美眼」を意味する場合がある。「味覚」を意味する場合には形容詞 tasteful は使われないが、「審美眼」を意味する場合には tasteful は「趣味のよい」という意味で用いられると解説する。続けてハーンは taste を使った表現の例として、"to show taste in/by"「～にセンスを示す」と "to have a taste for"「～に興味がある」を挙げ、その意味の違いと共に、後者には不定冠詞が付くことに注意させている。細やかな語彙指導を行っていたことが分かる。

ハーンはさらに、語と語の共起関係、すなわちコロケーションにも再三注意するように述べている。「間違いを犯す」という英語を使う際には "to make wrong" ではなくて "to do wrong" を使うと説明し、wrong という単語には do という動詞が共起の関係にあることに触れる。実際に言語を運用する上で必要不可欠なのがコロケーションなのだが、学習者は日本語の単語一つ一つにそれぞれ対応する英単語を組み合わせて"英訳"しがちなために、間違った英語になってしまう。このコロケーションに着目して語彙習得を目指す英語教授法が、現在重視されており、2012 年に小学館から出版された『プログレッシブ英語コロケーション辞典』を代表に、コロケーションに着目した多くの単語帳が出版されている。『コーパス 100 ！で英会話』など、NHK の語学番組でも、その回のテーマの英単語と共起する単語上位 5 つを挙げて、コロケーションを意識した構成をとることが多い。明治時代、ハーンがすでにこのようなコロケーションや意味論を意識した語彙の説明を行っていたことは興味深い。

また、授業内で説明される事柄や例文はどれも当時の学生たちにとって身近なものが多く、実際の生活に基づいたものであった。お金について説明するときには、ハーンは paper-money「紙幣」には複数形が無いが、coin「硬貨」には複数形があり、金や銀は複数形にならないが銅は複数形になり「銅貨」という意味になることに触れる。続いて cash に「紙幣を小銭に換える」という意味があることに触れ、実際の買い物の場面でどのようにこの語を使うかを例に挙げる。そこでは買い物の際、何を買い、いくら払い、いくらがお釣りで返ってくるか、細かく場面が設定されており、非常に実践的で生き生きとした英語が用いられている。丁稚がお釣りを持って店主と客の所に駆け寄る場面などは、その光景が目に浮かぶようであり、学生が実際に使う場面を想定しやすいものであったと思われる。

また、mail「郵便」に関する語の説明をする際にも、熊本第五高等学校の学生になじみがある「熊本郵便局」を例にあげ、そこから mail「郵便物」の定義が「郵便局を通過する全ての手紙や本、新聞」であるということや、郵便物を配達する人のことは mail-carrier と呼び、郵便物を運ぶ列車は mail-train、蒸気船の場合は mail steamer と呼ぶことなど、語を派生させていく。続いて実際の郵便に関する表現を挙げながら、語の定着を図るのだが、そこでも "The Kyushu mail was delivered in Tokyo on Saturday."「九州からの郵便物が土曜日に東京で配達された」や、"The Tokyo mail is expected here this evening."「東京からの郵便物は今夜着くはずだ」など、学生が普段の生活で用いるであろう文ばかりが例としてあげられている。これにより学生は、どのような場面でそれらの語を使うか容易に想像でき、語彙に対しての理解が深まるだけでなく、授業内でハーンが板書したそれらの表現を学生が口に出し何度も練習したことが予想される。このような実際に日常で用いられる英語表現は、まさに今の英語教育において教育者と学習者たちの双方が共に修得することを目標としている「生きた英語」であると言える。

　一方で、言葉の語源を重視することも、ハーンの授業の特徴である。例えば、"acolyte"「従者」という語については、「従者」を意味するギリシャ語の "acolouthos" が語源になっていることを説明し、同じように "sublime"「荘厳な」という語の説明をする際には、この語が「高尚」を意味するラテン語 "sublimis" から来ていることを学生に説明している。学習者が語彙を機械的に暗記する "rote learning" を行うことがないように、学生の語彙に対して興味を喚起している。そしてギリシャローマや、古英語の世界に遡る語源というルーツを知ることで、長い歴史の時間の中で言葉が生成してきたことを実感させることもまた、「生きている英語」の修得だとハーンは考えたのだろう。一つ一つの言葉を、意味の集積の総体としてハーンが捉えていたことがよくわかる。

　さらにハーンがあげる例文のなかには、ハーンだからこそと思えるようなものもあって興味深い。ハーンは例文として、西洋の古典的名作を多く取り上げている。たとえば、形容詞 "beautiful" の説明を行う際、ハーンは Alfred Tennyson(1809-1892) の *The Beggar Maid* という詩の一篇を引用する。この詩は女性に無関心であったアフリカの Cophetua 王が、乞食に身をやつしながらも目を見張るような美しさであった the beggar maid に一目で心を奪われ、彼女を妃として迎え、国民に愛されながら仲睦まじく暮らしたという伝説に基づくものだ。この伝説はいわば「シンデレラ・ストーリー」のようなものであり、古くは William Shakespeare の *Romeo and Juliet* で言及され、現代に至るまで多くの文学・絵画などにおいて登場した人気のあるものである。また、平川氏が序文で触れているように、夫の身代わりとなり若くして亡くなった Alkestis という女性にまつわるギリシャ悲劇も、授業の中で取り上げている。

　ハーンの前任者のお雇い外国人の英語教師がテキストとして George Eliot を取り上げていたように、当時の英語授業においては西洋の作家や思想家が書いた作品がテキストとしてよく用いられた。ハーンもまた Tennyson の詩を引用することにより、学生に西洋の文化に触れる機会を与え、その教養を深める助けをしているのだが、ハーンらしいと思えるのは、*The Beggar Maid* にせよ、Alkestis の物語にせよ、仮定法で用いられた鴛鴦の

とんち話にせよ、民話や神話伝説の範疇に入る作品を使っていることである。文化の違いを超えた普遍的な話型が見出せる物語だからこそ、学生たちの感性から離れすぎることなく、さらに比較文学的な関心をも引き出せると考えたに違いない。

　引用した作品だけではなく、語彙の説明自体にも、ハーンの感性を伺うことができる。例えば、sublime「荘厳（な）」という言葉について、人間がどういう場合に「荘厳な気持ち」になるのか、その例としてあげるのが、富士山、星空、嵐の海なのである。富士の高嶺を仰ぎ、満天の星空を見上げ、嵐の海を前にした時に、人は「荘厳な気持ち」になる。すなわち「半ば恐ろしく、半ば喜びに満ち、そして時にどこか物悲しい」感情を抱くのだが、それは偉大なる自然に対し人間という生き物が如何に小さく儚い存在であるかを痛感させられるからだとハーンは述べている。学生はこれらの説明を聞き、sublime という言葉の意味するところが、理屈ではなく、より感覚的に、イメージとして把握できたのではないだろうか。そしてエドモンド・バーク以来、ヨーロッパの詩学美学の思考の中心のひとつである「崇高」という概念についての理解の一助ともなったはずである。

　また、shade「陰」や shadow「影」という言葉を説明する際には、ハーンは shade という語の持つ興味深い点に触れる。shade は一般的に使われる「陰」という意味の他に、ghost「亡霊」や the spirit of a dead person「死者の魂」という意味を持つことや、死者の世界が The Shades と呼ばれると述べる。shade「陰」という一義的な訳語だけを与えるのではなく、そこから派生する「亡霊」や「死者の魂」のイメージについて言及するのである。学生の想像も、ふと語学の授業の枠を抜け出し、黄泉の国や死者の話にまで広がっていったかもしれない。『怪談』の著者ハーンらしい説明の仕方であると言えよう。

　ハーンはさらに日本と西洋との比較文化的な話題も取り上げている。family「家族」の説明では、日本と西洋の家族観の違いを述べているのが興味深い。例えば会話において"I have no family" と言った際、それは「私には妻子がいない」という意味であって、そこには両親や姉妹兄弟がいるかどうかは含まれないという。それゆえ「私には家族がいない」と言った際に日本語で想像されるような天涯孤独のイメージはそこにはない。また、西洋では子が親を扶養する義務も、一定年齢以上の子を親が扶養する慣習もないと述べて、西洋では、結婚をして自分の家庭を持つことが重要なのだと強調している。ハーンのこの説明を額面通りに、ただ単に東西の社会の違いの分析と受け取るのは、単純にすぎるかもしれない。ハーンは、日本の家族関係の長所や美徳について高く評価し、学生に向かってもそういう意見を述べていた。では、なぜハーン自身は家を捨てて、一人、遠い東洋の国にきて、ここで結婚したのか。熊本高校の大人びた青年たちの、ハーンを見る眼差しのなかに、口にこそしない素朴な疑問を、ハーンは読み取ったのかもしれない。西洋における親子関係の冷淡さを異常に強調する口調は、他の語彙の説明の調子とは、明らかに異なっている。松江の純朴な中学生相手には感じることのなかった、自らの過去への無言の問いかけに意図せず反論したものと考えてよいのではないか。そこに、ハーンの幼少時のトラウ

マの翳が伺える。ハーンは、そのあと続けて、長子相続制の話へと移る。イギリスの上流階級では、この長子相続の法律によって長男のみに財産が受け継がれ、次男以下の家を継がなかったものは家庭からはじき出され、アメリカや植民地に渡ったことが説明される。日本でも明治のころには、華族や士族、平民に至るまで、長男に家督が受け継がれていた。西洋の長子相続制の話は決して学生たちにとって遠い国の話ではなく、自分たちにとって親近感のわく、ともすれば身につまされる話題だったはずだ。比較文化的な視点が授業にもたらされることで、学生の興味はより喚起され、この話題が学生の目には印象深く映ったことと思われる。と同時に、このことを長々と口述したハーンの脳裏に、ギリシャからアイルランド、アメリカへと渡っていった自分の人生の軌跡が去来したことが想像される。

　最後に、友枝ノート（『ラフカディオ・ハーンの英語教育──友枝高彦・高田力・中土義敬のノートから』に収録）におけるハーンの授業との違いを指摘しておきたい。友枝ノートでは対象となる学年が旧制中学校第4学年（満16歳前後）であったのに対し、こちらの黒板ノートでは旧制高等学校第3学年（満20歳前後）に対する英語授業であったことから、友枝ノートの内容と比べると、文法的な説明や語法についての解説がより多くなっていることが分かる。

　そのなかで、仮定法の解説は友枝ノートでも行われており、ハーンが重要な文法事項と考えていたことが分かる。説明には友枝ノートと同じく、鵞鳥と狐を連れ、穀物の袋を持った男の愉快な話が使われている。男は川をボートで渡ろうとするのだが、ボートは小さすぎて持っているものを一つずつしか運ぶことができない。もし鵞鳥と穀物を一緒においておいたなら、鵞鳥は穀物を食べてしまうが、もし狐を鵞鳥と一緒においておいたなら、狐は鵞鳥を食べてしまうだろう。男はこれらの事態を回避するために、一体どのようにして川を渡ったのだろうか、という問いかけが為されるのだが、これはある種のゲームのようなものである。単に仮定法の文をいくつも羅列するのではなく、学生自身が頭を使い授業に参加する例文を用いることで、学生の関心を失うことなく仮定法の導入を行うことができていると言える。

　次に、友枝ノートには記述がない文法事項が、否定の付加疑問文や否定疑問文であり、ハーンは例文を多く出しながら、その解説をたいへん細かく行っている。否定の付加疑問文や否定疑問文とは、通常の「〜ですか？」という疑問文に対し、「〜ではないのですか？」という、否定の意味が込められている疑問文のことである。例えば"You have not written any composition for me, have you?"「あなたは僕のための作文をまだ何も書いていないんですね？」という否定の付加疑問文の場合、その答え方は"Yes, I have."「いいえ、書きましたよ」と"No, I haven't"「はい、書いていません」の二通りとなる。日本人学習者が苦手とするのは、質問者の「書いていないのか？」という疑問に対し「書いた」と答えたい場合、英語では"Yes"と答えるが、日本語では「いいえ」と答えることで、否定の意味を持つ疑問文に対する答え方は日本語と英語では真逆になるため、混乱す

ることが多い。しかしハーンはここで、非常に的確ですっきりとした解説を行う。つまり、日本人は疑問文に応える時、質問文それ自体に対し答えているのに対し、英語話者は自分が答える事実そのものに対して「肯定」か「否定」を述べると指摘する。それゆえ、先ほどの"You have not written any composition for me, have you?"という疑問文に対して、日本人の場合は、質問者の「書いていないのか？」という疑問それ自体を否定しているので「いいえ、書いた」となり、英語話者の場合は、自分の動作が「書いた」という肯定的なものであるので"Yes"と答えるのだ。質問に応える者が示す事実そのものに注意し、それが肯定文であれば"Yes"、否定文であれば"No"と答えればよい、というハーンの明快な指示により、学生は混乱することなくこの文法事項を学習できたと思われる。

　ラフカディオ・ハーンの英語の授業は、学生が興味を持てるような身近な素材を使いながら、母国語話者ならではの微妙なニュアンスの違いや単語のコロケーションを細かく指導するものであり、現代の英語教授法を先取りしたかのような趣がある。そこにさらにハーンらしい素材の提示や、比較文学的な要素が加えられて、授業がいっそう厚みを持ったものになっていたと言える。ハーンが松江でも熊本でも学生に慕われた大きな理由は、実はこのような深みのある英語授業にあったに違いない。100年以上も前に行われた、明治25年のハーンの授業は、ノートの冒頭で市河三喜が「一読スベキモノナリ」と記したように、現代の我々にとっても非常に魅力的なものであると言えよう。

（成城学園高等学校　外国語科講師）

熊本五高生・黒板勝美のハーン授業ノート
自筆原版・復元・日本語訳

黒板勝美

Idiom ニ二種アリ Common idiom, Literary idiom ナリ Literary idiom ハ時トシ Special meaning ヲ有スルニヨリ好ンテ之ヲ用ヰルコトアシ Common idiom ハ之ヲ適当ニ用ヰル時ハ文ヲ飾漂シ大ニ愛スルコトモノ文トナル可シ

Spontaneity.

一讀スベキモノナリ J.主

Idiom ニ二種アリ Common idiom, Literary idiom　是ナリ Literary idiom ハ時トシテ Special meaning ヲ有スルニヨリ好ンデ之ヲ用キルコト勿レ　Common idiom ハ之ヲ適當ニ用キル時ハ　文簡潔大ニ愛ス可キノ文トナル可シ

　　　Sponteneity*

<u>一読スベキモノナリ</u>　I. 生

慣用句に二種あり。一般的な慣用句・文語的な慣用句である。文語的な慣用句は時に特別な意味を有するので、好んでこれを用いることなかれ。一般的な慣用句はこれを適当に用いる時は、文簡潔大いに愛すべき文となるべし

無理のない自然さ

---

* Spontaneity

高美文筆記ハ余進卒第五高等
中学ニあり比ラフカヂオ、ヘルン(小泉
八雲)氏の口模さをとらろ今ヨ
てれと讀むも猶興味深し
なると覚ゆ
大正十二年九月廿有二夕
勝美記

この英文筆記ハ　余　熊本第五高等中学にありし比　ラフカヂオ・ヘルン（小泉八雲）氏の口授するところ　今にしてこれを　読むも　猶　興味津々たるを　覚ゆ

大正十二年九月廿有一日夕

勝美記

Conversation.

1. New Year.

TO PAY New Year's CALLS.
TO MAKE " "
AT New Year's (this covers the whole period of celebration).
   TO Exchange the compliments of the season.
      The compliments of the Season are —
"I wish you a Happy New Year." or 3 words only
    are used.
"The same to you, — and many of them."
TO have amusement, TO Play the game of cards.
Rule (general).
   Several — is used in the meaning of number of the same
    kind. "We played several games of football —
    i.e. the same game several times over.
   Different — is used in the meaning of number NOT of
    the same kind. "We played different games
    of cards — i.e. games of different kind.
   I spent the time in making pleasant visits to
    such places as —. I went hare-hunting.
Idioms — "For curiosity we started at night." or
    "For curiosity's sake."
    "I went there for health" or
    "I went there to recruit my health."

Conversation

1. New Year .

TO PAY New Year's <u>CALLS.</u>

TO MAKE 〃 〃 　　〃 .

AT New Year's (this covers the whole period of celebration.)

TO Exchange the <u>Compliments of the Season.</u>

　　　The Compliments of the Season are —

"I wish you a Happy New Year." or 3 words only
　　are used.

"The same to you,— and many of them."

To have amusement.　To PLay* the game of cards.

Rule (general).

　Several — is used in the meaning of number of <u>the same
　　kind.</u>　"We played several games of football" –
　　i.e. the same game several times over.

Different — is used in the meaning of number NOT of
　the same kind. "We played different games
　of cards — i.e. games of different kind.

I spent the time in making pleasant visits to
　such places as — .　I went hare- hunting.

Idioms: — "For curiosity we started at night." or
　　　　"For curiosity's sake."
　　　　"I went there <u>for health</u>" or
　　　　"I went there <u>to recruit my health.</u>"

---

* PLay=Play

会話

１．新年

年始の挨拶にうかがう

年始の挨拶にうかがう

新年に（この語は正月の期間全てをいう）

時候の挨拶を交わす

時候の挨拶とは—

「新年お慶び申し上げます」もしくは、三語のみ (Happy New Year) が用いられる。

「おめでとうございます、一幾久しくおめでとうございます」

娯楽を楽しむ。カードゲームをする。（花札で遊ぶ）

ルール（一般的なもの）

Several —同じ種類のものの数という意味で使用される。「私たちはフットボールの試合を数試合した。」—すなわち、繰り返し同じ競技の試合のこと

Different—同じ種類でないものの数という意味で使用される。「私たちは様々なカードゲームをした」—すなわち、異なる種類のゲームのこと

私は—のような場所を訪れて楽しく過ごした。兎狩りに行った。

熟語：—「好奇心に駆られて夜更けに出発した」もしくは
　　「好奇心を満たすために。」
　　「健康のためにそこに行った。」もしくは
　　「健康を回復するためにそこに行った。」

climb ⎫ a hill.
mount ⎬ a stairs.
ascend ⎭ a mountain, a tree.

climb ⎫ on a roof. ⎫ in these cases there is
mount ⎬ on a platform. ⎬ the idea of a level surface
ascend ⎭ upon a throne ⎭ to be reached.

mount a horse, mount ON horseback.
The word "climb down" denotes the action of hands and feet in descending like that of ascending (climb up).

2. **Æsthetic words.**

(1) taste — the sense which enables us to distinguish
(physical) the quality of food. This noun has NO corresponding adjective.

(2) taste — the intellectual sense which enables us
(moral) to distinguish what is beautiful, correct, or proper in art, in customs, and in intercourse.
   TASTEFUL (adj)
Accordingly the adjective TASTEFUL never refers to food. In speaking of food we say "sweet", "bitter", "toothsome", "agreeable", &c; but never "tasteful".

climb	a hill	
mount	a stairs	
ascend	a mountain, a tree	
climb	<u>on</u> a roof.	in these cases there is
mount	<u>on</u> a platform.	the idea of a level surface
ascend	<u>upon</u> a throne	to be reached

mount a horse,   mount ON horseback.
The word "climb <u>down</u>" denotes the action of hands
 and put in descending like that of ascending
(climb <u>up</u>).

2. <u>Æsthetic words</u>
(1) taste — the sense which enables us to distinguish
(physical)   the quality of food. This noun has NO corresponding adjective.

(2) taste — the intellectual sense which enables us
(moral)   to distinguish what is beautiful, correct, or proper
            in art, in custom, and in intercourse.
            TASTEFUL (adj.)

Accordingly the adjective TASTEFUL <u>never</u> refer* to food.
In speaking of food we say "sweet," "bitter," " toothsome,"
"agreeable," &c, but <u>never</u>" tasteful."

---

* refers

Idioms of TASTEFUL & TASTE.
 "TO SHOW taste {in/of} — ex. "He showed taste in his selection of pictures." "He showed his good taste by refusing to buy the statue."
 "TO have A taste FOR — ex. "He has a taste for drawing." "He has a taste for pictures."
TASTEFUL and its adverb.
ex. "His books are tastefully bound."
 "His dress is tasteful." (correct and nice)
 "The room was tastefully arranged for the reception of guests."
 "The decorations were ample and cheap, but very tasteful."

Pleasing

Pretty — always conveys the idea of smallness, tenderness. Therefore especially used in relation to small things, and small people or animals, and children.
Beautiful — This word is of unlimited application to large things, or even small things admir—
× consequently it is highly insulting to call a man pretty.

Idioms of TASTEFUL & TASTE

" TO SHOW taste {IN or BY} — Ex. "He showed taste in his selection of pictures. He showed his good taste by refusing to buy the statue.
" TO have A taste FOR — Ex. "He has a taste for drawing." He has a taste for pictures."

TASTEFUL and its adverb.
EX. "His books are tastefully bound."
"His dress is tasteful," (correct and nice.)
"The room was tastefully arranged for the reception of gests*.
The decorations were simple and cheap but very tasteful.

 Pleasing

Pretty — always conveys the idea of smallness, tenderness. Therefore especially used in relation to small things, and small people or animals, and children. ※

Beautiful — This word is of unlimited application to large things, or even small things admir-

※ consequently it is highly insulting to call a man pretty.

---

* guests

TASTEFUL と TASTE の慣用句
・〜にセンスを示す　一例)「彼が選んだ絵画に、彼のセンスの良さが表れている。」「彼はその彫像を買うことを拒否したことにより、審美眼があることを示した。」
・〜に興味がある　一例)「彼は絵を描くことが好きだ。」「彼は絵画に興味がある。」

TASTEFUL とその副詞
例)「彼の本は趣味良く装丁されている。」
「彼の服装は上品だ。」(礼儀にかなっていて、趣味が良い)
「その部屋は客人をもてなすために、趣味良く整えられていた。」
「その装飾は簡素で安価なものながら、非常に趣味が良かった。」

Pleasing　—　心地良い

Pretty　—　常に小ささ、優しさ、という概念を示唆する。
したがって、小さいものや、小さい人や動物、子供に関して用いられる。※

Beautiful　—　この語は大きいものから精巧に作られた小さいものにまで制限無く使える。

※したがって、男性を pretty と呼ぶことは非常に侮辱的である。

ably made. It can be used for the day, the sky, moonlight, colour, nights, and extraordinary perfection of body.

    In robe and crown and crown
        The King stepped down
    To meet and greet her on her way
    "It is no wonder," said the lords,
    "She is more beautiful than day." — Tennyson;
                       King Cophetua

Graceful — Refers to perfection of motion and proportion of a special kind. Grace requires great slenderness joined with great strength and activity.

    "The bamboo is graceful — not the pine."
    "The deer is graceful — not the cow."

In scientific language "grace" means "The ECONOMY of forces" — the greatest possible result with the smallest possible amount of material. Therefore the words always conveys to the mind its outward sign — slender proportion and balance.

Sublime — noble, (lofty, deep) solemn, any of these
    (Latin sublimis "lofty.")

ably made. It can be used for the day, the sky, moonlight, colour, nights, and extroadinary perfection of body.

In robe and crown and crown*¹
    the King stepped down
To meet and greet her on her way
"It is no wonder," said the lords.
    "She is more <u>beautiful</u> than day" —— Tennyson,
        King Cophetua

Graceful — Refers to per~~don~~ of motion and pro-^fection portion of a <u>special</u> kind. Grace requires great slenderness joind*² with great strength and activity.

"The bamboo is graceful — not the pine."
The deer is graceful — not the cow.

In scientific language "grace" means "The ECONOMY of Forces"— The greatest possible result with the smallest possible amount of material.

Therefore the words*³ always ~~covers~~ to the mind ^conveys
its outward sign – slender proportion and balance.

Sublime — noble, {lofty}{deep} solemn, any of these
    (Latin sublimis "lofty")

---

*1 and crown 間違って二回書き写した
*2 joined
*3 word

太陽や空、月の光、色、夜、また極めて完成された肉体にも用いられうる。

王冠と袍衣をつけた
王は下りて
道で彼女に逢って会釈せられた
「不思議はない、あの女は陽よりも美しい」と殿様達は言った¹　—アルフレッド・テニスン
    King Cophetua

Graceful　—　動作や見た目の均整が完ぺきで、一種特別であることを言う。優美さは、大いなるしなやかさと共に強い力と活発さを併せ持つことを必要とする。

「竹は優美である―松はそうではない。」
「鹿は優雅である―牛はそうではない。」
科学用語では、"grace" とは「力のエコノミー」を意味する。— つまり、できるだけ最小限の資材で、最大限の結果を得ること
したがって、この単語はつねに外見上の特徴―ほっそりとした体格や均整―を想起させる。

Sublime　—　この語には気高さ、高尚、深さ、厳粛など
  （「高尚」を表わすラテン語 sublimis から）

---

1 アルフレッド・テニスン『テニスン小曲集』幡谷正雄訳、交蘭社、大正 14 年。

ideas may be contained in the word.
Mount Fuji is one sublime thing in Nippon.
The sky on a clear starry night.
The sea in a storm.

Why should such sight make us solemn,— half-afraid and half-delighted: sometimes half-sad.

When we look at a stupendous range of mountains, for example, we feel sad, however beautiful the scenery. Because, all unconsciously we feel that what we see is eternal, and that our own bodies are short. Besides there comes to us the idea of the enormous force that produced those mountains, and that idea brings with it the idea of fear.

Since a poem which awakens feelings of the same kind may be called sublime. Or a work of art.

As man's mind developed through scientific knowledge, his ideas became too large to be expressed by old words. New words have been invented. COSMIC EMOTION is a term used

ideas <u>may</u> be contained in the word.
Mount Fuji is one sublime thing in Nippon.
The sky on a clear starry night
The sea in a storm.

———

Why should such sight make us solemn, — half-afraid and half-delighted: sometimes half-sad.

When we look at a stupendous range of mountains, for example, we feel sad, however beautiful the scenery.   Because, all unconsciously we feel that what we see is eternal, and that our own bodies are short. Besides there comes to us the idea of the enormous force that produced those mountains, and that idea brings with it the idea of fear.

Hence a poem which awakens feelings of the same kind may be called sublime.
Or a work of art.

As man's mind developed* through scientific knowledge, his ideas become too large to be expressed by old words. New words have been invented, COSMIC EMOTION is a term used

———

*develops

こういった概念が含まれうる。
富士山は、日本における荘厳なものの一つである。
澄みわたった満天の星空
嵐の海

———

なぜこのような景色は我々を荘厳な気持ち―半ば恐ろしく、半ば喜びに満ちた、そして時にどこか物悲しいそんな感情を呼び起こすのだろう。

たとえば、我々が並外れて巨大な山脈を見た時、美しい景色ではあるが、悲しい気持ちになる。なぜならば、我々は全く無意識のうちに、我々が見ているものは永遠に続くが、我々の肉体は儚いものだと感じるからである。さらに、それらの山々を創りだした巨大な力の概念が我々の心に浮かび、その考えが畏怖の念をもたらす。

それゆえに、そのような感情をもたらす詩は sublime（崇高な）と呼ばれることもある。芸術作品の場合もそうである。

人間の精神は、科学的知識とともに発達してきたので、その思想は古い言葉で表わすには大きくなりすぎた。新しい言葉が作り出され、COSMIC EMOTION（宇宙的感情）という言葉が

by the mathematician Clifford to describe the loftiest feeling of modern man. Emotions given us by the comprehension of a Universal Law are thus called, — or emotions caused by the recognition of something beautiful in <u>all human nature</u> — not in one person only.

(3.) <u>Use</u> of polite phrases in conversation.
"<u>Please</u> lend me your book" is much more polite form than
"Lend me your book, <u>please</u>" except in speaking to servants
<u>please</u> ought always to go first.
But such forms of expression are not the <u>most</u> polite.

"Would you be so kind as to lend me your book?"
In very polite language we avoid the use of WILL and SHALL as much as possible.
Ex. Would you like tea or coffee? | Would you do me the favor to call on me to-day?
Which <u>would</u> you prefer — tea or coffee? | May I have the pleasure of asking you to dine?

by the mathematician Clifford to describe the loftiest feeling of modern man. Emotion given us by the comprehension of a Universal Law are thus called, — or emotions caused by the recognition of something beautiful <u>in all human</u> nature — not in one person only.

(3) <u>Use</u> of polite-phrases in Conversation
　　"<u>Please</u> lend me your book" is much more polite form than
　　"Lend me your book, <u>please</u>." except in speaking to servants.
　　　　<u>please</u> ought always to go first.
But such forms of expression are not the <u>most</u> polite.

　　Would you be so kind as to lend me your book?
In very polite language we avoid the use of WILL and SHALL as much as possible.

| Ex. "Would you like tea or coffee? Which <u>would</u> you <u>prefer</u>, tea or coffee? | <u>Would</u> you do me the favor to call on me today? <u>May</u> I have the pleasure of asking you to dine? |

現代人の最も崇高な感情を表現するために数学者のCliffordによって用いられた。宇宙の法則に対する理解によってもたらされる感情、または、一個人ではなく<u>人間すべてに備わる本性</u>の何か美しいものを認識した際に、生み出される感情がこのように呼ばれる。

(3) 会話における敬語の使用
　"Please lend me your book（あなたの本を貸してくださいませんか）"は
　"Lend me your book, please（あなたの本を貸してください）"よりずっと丁寧であるが、使用人に対して使う場合は除く。
　pleaseという語は常に先頭に来るべきである。
　しかし、これらの表現法は最も丁寧なものではない。

　あなたの本を貸していただけませんでしょうか？
非常に丁寧な表現の場合、willやshallの使用はなるべく避ける。

| 例）「お茶かコーヒーはいかがですか？」「お茶かコーヒー、どちらがよろしいですか？」 | 「今日我が家にいらっしゃいませんか」「お食事にお誘いしてもよろしいですか？」 |

"Could you do me the favour lending me that paper?"
"Would you be so kind good as to tell me the way to Blank street?"

For the same reasons the conditional form is also used in expressing one's own will or desire. Never say to a stranger "I wish," or "I want you to —"

"I would like tea to have some tea?"
"I would like to know ——"
"I wish to know —" (only by a master to a servant.)
"If you would be so kind ——"
"If you could be so kind as to lend it to you, I will be very grateful."

It would give us much pleasure to see you at our house.

(If we use WILL in the above circumstances, it would mean that we felt quite certain the person would come. But to express certainty about the actions of another is impolite.)

<u>Could</u> you do me the favour lending me that paper? good.
<u>Would</u> you be so kind as to tell me the way to Blank street?

For the same reasons the conditional form also
is used in expressing one's own will or desire.   Never say to a <u>stranger</u>.
"I <u>wish</u>," or "I <u>want</u> you to
"I <u>would</u> like ~~tea~~ to have some tea?"
"I would like to know —."
"I wish to know"— (only by a master to a servant.)
"If you <u>would</u> be so kind —
"If you <u>could</u> be so kind as to lend 100 yen, I <u>will</u> be very grateful.

It would give us much pleasure to see you at our house.
　　(If we use WILL in the above circumstances, it would mean that we felt quite certain the person would come. But to express certainty about the actions of another is impolite.

そちらの紙を貸し<u>ていただけますか</u>？
ブランク通りまでの道を教え<u>ていただけますか</u>？

同じ理由により、仮定法の形式もまた個人の意思や欲求を伝える際に用いられる。決して見知らぬ人に
"I <u>wish</u>" や "I <u>want</u> to は言ってはならない。
「お茶を<u>頂きたい</u>のですが？」
「—を知りたいのですが。」
「—について知りたい」—（主人が使用人に使う場合のみ）
「もし御親切にも—」
「もし御親切にも 100 円貸していただけましたら、非常にありがたく思います。」

「もし我が家に来ていただければ、とても嬉しく思います」
　（もし上記の状況で Will を使うと、相手が必ず来ると思っていることを意味する。しかしながら、他人の行動を確信を持って表現することは、失礼にあたる）

"Would you give me the pleasure of your company at dinner?" or — (better)
"May I have the pleasure of your company at dinner?"

In writing we would say:
— "We hope to have the pleasure of your company at dinner."

this only at the end of English letters
{
I remain, dear Sir,
Your very humble and Obedient Servant
So and So.
}

Today, it is better to say
Faithfully
———

May I have the pleasure of knowing your name?

May I take the liberty of asking for your address?

May I have the HONOR of knowing your name? (to a lady) - not to a man unless a very great person.

"Would you give me the pleasure of your company at dinner ? "   or — (better)
"May I have the pleasure of your company at dinner?"
In writing we would say :
— "We hope to have the pleasure of your company at dinner.

             I remain, dear Sir,
This only at the   your very humble and
end of English   obedient Servant
letters   So and so.

       Today, it is better to say,
               Faithfully

  May
~~Might~~ I have the pleasure of knowing your name?
May I take the liberty of asking for your <u>address</u>?
May I have the HONOUR of knowing your name? (to a lady) — not to a
             very
man unless a great person.

「夕食においでいただけますか？」
もしくは―（こちらの方が良い）
「夕食においでいただけませんでしょうか？」
手紙に書くときには、
―「夕食においで頂けることを楽しみにしております。」

このような表現はイギリスの手紙の末尾でしか用いられない。

親愛なる閣下の賤しく忠実なる僕であります、云々／だれそれ

今日では、Faithfully と言う方が好ましい。

「お名前を伺ってもよろしいですか？」
「ぶしつけながら、ご住所を伺ってもよろしいですか？」
「おそれながら、お名前を頂戴してもよろしいですか？」（女性に対して）
　―よほど偉い人でなければ男性には用いない。

The anniversary of the accession to the throne of the Emperor Jimmu.

His Majesty the present Emperor is the lineal descendant of the Emperor Jimmu, and his 122nd successor.

past	present	future
ancestors	descendants	Posterity

Imperator = A Roman Supreme — military commander. hence our strong adj: "Imperious."
"Imperative."

The Tsar or Czar; from Cæsar.
Kaiser
Kaisar-i-Hind (Arabian word) — Empress of India

The Imperial Crest (mon).

crest.   Coat of arms   Crest & Lamb. Arms of Spain

The 2 lion signified Leon, in Spain
The 2 castle, Castille
The Lamb, an Order established by Charles I.

The anniversary of the accession to the throne of the Emperor Jimmu

His Majesty the present Emperor is the lineal descendant of the Emperor of Jimmu, and his 122nd successor.

past	present	future
ancestors	descendants	Posterity

Impirator*1 = A Roman Supreme — military [commander

hence our strong adj. "Imperious," "Imperative."

The Tsar or Czar } from Caesar
Kaiser

Kaisar-i-Hind (Arabian word) — Emperor (ress) of India

The Imperial Crest (mon)

Crest    lion — Coat-of-arms   Castle lion / Leon Castille — Crest of Lamb, Arms of Spain

The 2*2 lion signified Leon, in Spain
The 2*2 castle, Castille
The Lamb, an Order established by [Charles V.

---

*1 Imperator
*2 2nd

神武天皇紀元節

今上天皇は神武天皇の直系の子孫にあたり、百二十二番目の継承者である。

過去	現在	未来
先祖	末裔	後代の人々

Imperator（皇帝）— 古代ローマの最高権力者 — 軍の総司令官

　それゆえ、"Imperious（威厳のある）""Imperative（命令形）"という強い意味を持つ形容詞がある

The Tsar もしくは
Czar（ツァーリ）   } Caesar（カエサル）が語源
Kaiser（皇帝）

Kaisar-i-Hind（アラビア語）— インド皇帝（女帝）

帝国の紋章（紋）
たてがみ→紋章の頂飾　　盾形の紋章

スペインの紋章
羊の紋飾り

二つめのライオンはスペインのレオン（十世紀ごろから存在した王国）を、
二つめの城は Castille（カスティリヤ王国）を表わした
この Lamb はカール五世によって制定された（スペインの）金羊毛勲章のこと。

The term "Arms" or "Coat-of-Arms" are survivals from feudalism, when these things were really painted upon the armour or shield.

The crest, stamped beside the signature of a ~~title~~ letter, or other public document, is ~~read~~ called the Seal.

Light and Shadow.

The light) Sunlight
of the sun) Sunshine

Sun — as in the phrase "to stand in the sun" most commonly used in conversation.

Sunbeam — a ray of sunlight
a beam — a straight line of light.

in the sun | in the shade

"Let us get in the shade; it is too hot in the sun."

Shade — a general term for space covered by shadow — protected from the sun. Collective shadow.

Shadow — The silhouette, or shadow-shape of one object.

46

The term "Arms" or "Coat-of-Arms" are survivals from feudalism, when these things were really painted upon the armour or shield
The crest stamped beside the signature of a ~~title~~ letter, or other public document, is ~~coal~~ called the Seal.

    Light and Shadow
The light | Sunlight
of the sun | Sunshine
    Sun — as in the phrase "to stand in the sun" most commonly used in conversation.

Sunbeam — a ray of sunlight
a beam — a straight line of light

  in the sun | in the shade
"Let us get in the shade; it is too hot in the sun"
Shade — a general term for space covered by shadow — protected from the sun
    Collective shadow
Shadow – The silhouette, or shadow — shape of one object.

"Arms" や "Coat-of Arms" という語は封建制度の遺物であり、これらは甲冑や盾の上に実際に描かれていた。
　紋章は手紙やその他公的な書類に書かれたサインの横にも押され、Seal（印章）と呼ばれた。

光と影
太陽の光　|　日光
　　　　　|　日差し
　Sun（太陽） — 「日向（ひなた）に立つ」という慣用表現にあるように最も一般的な会話の中では the sun と定冠詞づきで用いられる。
Sunbeam（太陽光線） — 日光の太陽光線
a beam（光線） — 光がさすそのまっすぐな線

日向で　　　　|　日陰で
「日陰にはいろう、日向は暑すぎる」
Shade（陰） — 影になっている場所を指す一般的な語—日差しから守られている場所
　　　　　複数の影の集合体
Shadow（影） — シルエット、影
　　　　　一つの物体の輪郭線

47

A very curious exception is furnished by the ancient word SHADE, signifying a Ghost, or the Spirit of a dead person. Used especially in speaking of the dead of the Greeks and Romans. And the world of the dead was called The Shades.

But the shape of objects as seen in still water, in polished metal, or in a looking-glass, are never called Shadows but REFLECTION.

Except in the use of the word shade for ghost, the words shade and shadow always imply darkness, blackness.

"The white shades of the dead."

A condition of indistinctness, between light and darkness — is spoken of as DIM.

"A dim religious light."

"A dull day, a dull light."

relation to idea of weariness of mind.   relation to idea of edge.

On the other hand, we have the beautiful word VIVID, used to describe colours and beauty of objects. It has the sense of "living" but living in

A very curious exception is furnished by
the quaint word. SHADE, signifying a Ghost
or the Spirit of a dead person. Used especially
in speaking of the dead of the Greeks and Romans.
And the world of the dead was called The
Shades.

But the shapes of objects as seen in still
water, in polished metal, or in a looking-
glass are never called Shadows but
REFLECTION.
 Except the use of the word shade for ghost,
the words shade and shadow — always imply in
darkness, blackness.
 "The white shades of the dead."

 of indistinctness,
A condition between light, and darkness —
is spoken of as DIM.
 "A dim religious light."
  "A dull day,   a dull light"
   relation to idea of   relation to idea of edge.
    weariness of mind
On the other hand, we have the beautiful word
VIVID, used to describe colours and beauty of
objects. It has the sense of "living" but living in

非常に興味深い例外があり、このShadeという面白い単語は亡霊や死者の魂を表わす。特にギリシャ人やローマ人の死者について話す時に用いられる。
また、死者の世界はThe Shadesと呼ばれていた。

しかし、静かな水面や磨き上げられた金属面、姿見にうつる物体の姿形はShadowとは決して呼ばず、Reflection（反射）と呼ぶ。

　亡霊の意味でShadeという語を用いる場合を除くとShadeやShadowという単語は一常に暗闇や黒さを含意する。
「死んだ人たちの白い亡霊」
光と暗闇の中間の茫漠とした状態は―
Dim（薄暗い）と呼ばれる。
「ぼんやりとした宗教の光」
「どんよりとした日、　　　にぶい光」
退屈している心理状態の連想から　刀などの切れ味の連想から

一方で、Vivid（鮮やかな）という美しい単語も存在しものの色彩や美しさを表現するのに用いられる。この語は「生きている」という感覚を有するものであるが

49

the strongest and best sense.
"How vivid everything seems to say!"
"The shadows are growing long"
"It is evening."
And the phrase "evening shadows" may often be found in <u>literature</u>.

The word "large" always contains the idea of BROAD as well as the idea of high. Especially broad

Some uses of the conditional

There was a countryman who had a pet goose, a pet fox, and a bag of corn. He wanted to take them across a river in a boat. But the boat was so small that he could take over only 1 at a time. He was anxious. For if he left the goose alone with the corn, the goose would eat the corn; and if he left the fox alone with the goose the fox would eat the goose. What did he do?

He first took the goose over. Then

the strongest and best sense.
 "How vivid everything seems to say*!"
"The shadows are growing long"
       It is evening.
And the phrase "evening shadows" may often
 be formed in Literature.
        ———————

The word "large" always contains the idea of
BROAD as well as the idea of high. Especially
broad.

        Some uses of the conditional

   There was a countryman who ^had^ a pet goose,
a pet fox, and a bag of corn. He wanted
 to take them across a river in a boat.
But the boat was so small that he could
 take over only 1 at a time. He was anxious. For if he left the goose alone with
 the corn, the goose would eat the corn, and if
he left the fox alone with the goose the
 fox would eat the goose. What did
  he do?
   He first took the goose over. Then

————————————————————————————
* today

最も強く最も良い意味での「生きている」という感覚だ。
「今日は[2]なんて全てが色鮮やかに見えるのかしら！」
「影は長く伸びている」
       これは夕方のこと。
また "evening shadows"「夕闇」という表現は、文学作品においてしばしば用いられることがある
        ————————

"large" という言葉が意味するところには、高さと同様に幅の広さも常に含まれる。特に幅広さについて。

仮定法の使用例

　あるところに、鶩鳥と狐を連れ、穀物の袋を持った田舎男がいた。男はボートで川を渡ろうと思ったが、そのボートはとても小さく、持っているものを一つずつしか運ぶことができなかった。男は不安になった。なぜなら、もし鶩鳥と穀物を一緒に置いておいたなら、鶩鳥は穀物を食べてしまうだろうし、もし狐と鶩鳥を一緒に置いておいたなら、狐は鶩鳥を食べてしまうだろう。彼はどうしたであろうか？
　彼はまず、鶩鳥を連れて行った。

————————————————————————————
2 板書では to say とあるが、おそらく today の写し間違い

he took over the fox, and brought back the goose. Then he took over the bag of corn. And last of all, he took over the goose.

He was able to do this by reflecting that it was necessary to keep the fox and the corn together. For if he had left the fox and the goose together, or the goose & the corn together, — then the fox would have eaten the goose, or the goose the corn.

Cleopatra was able to do much mischief because she was very beautiful as well as very bad. So a philosopher says: — "If the nose of Cleopatra had been half an inch shorter, the history of the world would have been changed."

"A miss is as good as a mile," says an English proverb.
                                        Mark

| To miss | To hit |
| A miss | A hit |

he took over the fox, and brought back the goose. Then he took over the bag of corn. And last of all, he took over the goose

He was able to do this by reflecting that it was necessary to keep the fox and the corn together. For if he had left the fox and the goose together, or the goose & the corn together, — then the fox would have eaten the goose, or the goose the corn.

———

Cleopatra was able to do much mischief because she was very beautiful as well as very bad. So a philosopher says, —"If the nose of Cleopatra had been half an inch shorter, the history of the world would have been changed."

"A miss is as good as a mile," says an English proverb.

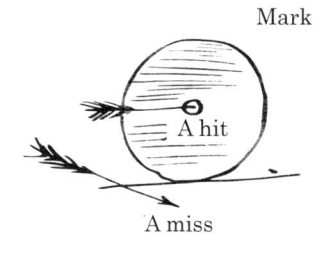

To miss	To hit
A miss	A hit

Mark
A hit
A miss

次に狐を連れて行って、鶩鳥を連れ帰った。そして穀物の袋を持っていき、最後に鶩鳥を連れて行った。

狐と穀物を一緒に置いておく必要があると考えたので、このような行動ができたのだ。というのも、もし彼が狐と鶩鳥、もしくは鶩鳥と穀物を一緒に置いてしまっていたら―そうしたら、狐は鶩鳥を、鶩鳥は穀物を食べてしまっていただろう。

———

クレオパトラは、非常に美しいだけでなく悪女でもあったので、大変な災いをもたらしてしまった。それゆえある哲学者にいわせると―もしクレオパトラの鼻が半インチ低かったなら、世界の歴史は変わっていただろう。

「少しの外れでも、外れは外れ」（ちょっと外れても、1マイル外れたのと同じ）はイギリスの諺である。

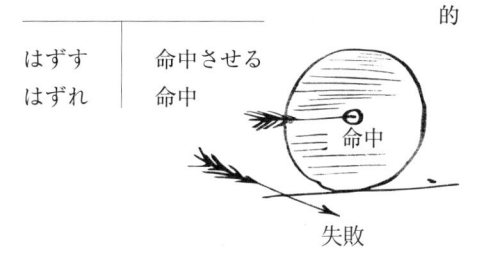

はずす	命中させる
はずれ	命中

的
命中
失敗

If the soldier who fired at Napoleon at Arcola had aimed an inch more to the left, the map of Europe would not be the same as it is now.

If Field-Marshall Von Moltoke had been killed at the beginning of the war with France in 1870 what would have been the probable result of the war? The French would been conquered. In other words, the probable result wd have been just the same.

"If," the word of conditional, is the subject of many proverbs in English. A student's proverb used to be, "IF stands stiff in the corner," That is, never accomplishes anything. But a conditional sentence can be formed without IF.

"If I had never read the story, I should still know the truth." Can be changed "Had I never _____." This form is often used in poetry.

If the soldier who fired at Napoleon at Arcole <u>had</u> <u>aimed</u> an inch more to the left, the map of Europe <u>would</u> not <u>be</u> the same as it is <u>now</u>.

If Field-Marshall Von Moltoke had been killed at the beginning of the war with France in 1870 what <u>would</u> <u>have</u> <u>been</u> the probable result of the war?　The French would*1 been conquered. In other words, the probable result <u>wd</u>*2 have been just the same.

　"If" the word of conditional, is the ~~same~~ subject of many proberbs*3 in English.　A student's proverb used to be "IF stands stiff in the corner," That is, never accomplishes anything. But a conditional sentence can be formed without IF.
　"If I had never read the story, I should still know the truth." can be changed "Had I never ──" This form is often used in poetry.

---

*1 have が入る
*2 would
*3 proverbs

もしアルコレでナポレオンに向かって発砲した兵士が、あと1インチ左を狙っていれば、ヨーロッパの地図は<u>今</u>と同じにはなっていない<u>だろう</u>。

もしフォン・モルトケ陸軍元帥が1870年のフランスとの戦いの序盤に殺されていたなら、戦争はどのような結果になっていただろうか？フランス人は負けていただろう。言い換えると、多分結果は全く同じだっただろう。

　"if" という仮定の言葉は、イギリスの多くの諺で主語になっている。
学生の諺で「「もし」は端っこから動かない[3]」というものがあるが、これはつまり、何も成し遂げない、という意味である。しかし、仮定法の文はIFを使わなくとも作ることができる。
「もし私がこの本を全く読んでいなかったとしても、それでも真実を知っただろう」という文章は、条件節を倒置して言い換えることができる。
この形式は詩作でしばしば用いられる。

---

3 "If stands stiff in a poor man's pocket." という諺もあり、これは「貧乏人は「もし―だったら」と仮定の話ばかりする」という意味。

to leave (verb) } There is no
leave (noun) } connection at
 all.
to leave — to go away, to bequeath by
 death, &c.
✱ leave — permission (sometimes
 farewell

Therefore the idiom TO TAKE LEAVE OF
"Please give me leave to get my
 book"____

"His eyes are bigger than his belly"
 (Said to a person who asks for more food
 than he can possibly eat.)
"He digs his grave with his teeth"
 (He is killing himself "gluttony")
"If you can't bite, never show your teeth"
 (Never threaten to do what you are not
 strong enough to do.
"Even the Devil is not so black as he is
 painted." (A man is always said to be
 worse than he is by his enemy. We must

to leave （verb） ⎫ There is no
leave （noun） ⎬ connection at
                ⎭ all.

to leave — to go away,　to bequeath by death, &c.

to leave — permission (sometimes farewell

Therefore the Idiom TO TAKE LEAVE OF
"Please give me leave to get my book" ———

"His eyes are bigger than his belly."
(Said to a person who asks for more food than he can possibly eat.)
"He digs his grave with his teeth"
(He is killing himself g^ulattony.)
"If you can't bite, never show your teeth."
 (Never threaten to do what you are not strong enough to do.
"Even the Devil is not so black as he is painted." (A man is always said to be worse than he is by his enemy. We must

---

去る（動詞）　｜ ここには何の関連もない
許可（名詞）　｜

to leave — 立ち去る、
　　　　　遺言でゆずる
leave — 許可
　　　（別れ、という意味にもなる）

従って、to take leave of ~（~に暇乞いをする）という慣用句がある
「私の本を取ってきてもよろしいでしょうか？」

「彼の目は彼の胃袋よりも大きい」
（自分が食べられる量よりも
多い量を欲しがる人のことをいう）
「彼は自らの歯で自分の墓穴を掘る」
（大食漢のあまり死に至る）
「もし噛みつくことができないのなら、歯を見せるな」
（自分がある行動ができるほど十分に強くないのなら、そうすると脅すな）
「悪魔でさえも絵に描かれるほど黒くはない」（人は、常に敵対者からは実際以上に悪く言われるものなので、

not believe the worst we hear.)
"When the Fox begins to preach, take care of your geese." (when a very cunning person begins to talk about honesty & virtue, that is the time to beware of him.)
"He is like a bull in a china-shop."
He is so clumsy that he breaks everything he touches.
"Walls have ears."
We cannot be too careful about not speaking of what we should not like everybody to know.
"The Road to Hell is paved with good intentions."
It is more easy to make good resolutions than to keep them. To make them & not to keep them, is what the wicked do.
"High regions are never without storms."
The greater a man's success in life the greater also his troubles & danger.
"If you have no enemies, Fortune has forgotten you."
"If you have one good friend, you have more than your share."

not b^e^lieve the worst we hear.)
"When the Fox begins to preach, take care of your geese." (when a very cunning person begins to talk about honesty & virtue, that is the tune to beware of him.)

"He is like a bull in a china-shop." He is so clumsy that he breaks everything he touches.

"Walls have ears." We cannot be too careful about not speaking ~~to~~ of what we should not like everybody to know.

"The Road to Hell is paved with good intention." It is more easy to make good resolution than to keep them. To make them & not to keep them, is what the wicked do.

"High regions are never without storms." The greater a man's success in life the greater also his ~~st~~ troubles & danger.

"If you have no enem^ies^, Fortune has forgotten you."

"If you have one good friend, you have more than your share."

悪いことを聞いても鵜呑みにしてはいけない。)
「狐が説教をし始めたら、鵞鳥を隠せ」
(非常にずる賢い奴が誠実さや美徳について語り出したら、そいつに注意しなくてはいけないという合図である)
「彼は瀬戸物屋の中にはいった牡牛のようだ」
彼はがさつな男で触れるものはなんでも壊してしまう
「壁に耳あり」
人に知られたくないことはしゃべらないように、どんなに注意しても、注意しすぎることは無い
「地獄への道は善意で敷き詰められている」[4]
良い決心をすることは、それを守って行動に移すよりも簡単なことである。良い約束をするだけでそれを実行しないというのは、悪人がすることだ。)
「高い場所には、必ず嵐が起こる」
人生において成功すればするほど、トラブルや危険というのもまた大きくなる
「もしあなたに敵がいなければ、運命の女神はあなたを忘れてしまったのだ」
「もしあなたに一人でも親友がいれば、それ以上のことはない」[5]

---

4 Samuel Johnson の格言
5 Thomas Fuller の格言

59

"Everybody's friend is nobody's friend."
 The man who tries to make himself liked by everybody – both good & bad – is not a sincere, but a cunning man.

"He who says what he likes, hears what he doesn't like."

"What's bred in the bone, comes out in the flesh."
 (A child born of vicious parents will show himself wicked or vicious sooner or later.)

"Faint heart never won fair lady."
 A cowardly man can never get a beautiful woman to marry him (literary). But the general meaning is that a coward can never get anything good.

"Love me little and love me long."
 (Extravagant affection never lasts.)

"If you want to know the value of money – just try to borrow some."

"Spare the rod and spoil the child."
 The parents who really love their child, must not neglect to punish it when necessary. A child who is never punished becomes selfish.

"Everybody's friend is nobody's friend."
　The man who tries to make himself
　liked by everybody — both good & bad —
　is not a sincere ,but a cunning man.
"He who says what he likes, hears what
　he doesn't like."
"What's bred in the bone, comes out
　in the flesh."
"(A child born of vicious parents will show
　himself wicked or vicious sooner or later.)
"Faint heart never won fair lady."
　A cowardly man can never get a beautiful
　　woman to marry him (literary). But
　the general meaning is that a coward
　can never get anything good.
"Love me little and love me long."
　(Extravagant affection never lasts.)
"If you want to know the value of
　money — just try to borrow some.
"Spare the rod and spoil the child."
　The parents who really love their child,
　must not neglect to punish it when
　necessary. A child who is never punish*
　becomes selfish.

---

* punished

「皆の友達は、誰の友達でもない」
　誰からも、良い人間からも悪い人間からも、好かれようとする人間は、誠実な人間ではなく、ずる賢い人間だ。
「自分が好きなことばかり言う者は、自分が嫌なことも聞かされる」
「親譲りの性格は必ず現れる」
（悪人の両親から産まれた子供は、遅かれ早かれ、悪さをするようになるだろう）
「弱気な心では美人を得たためしがない」
　臆病な男は決して美しい女性を娶ることはできない（字義通りの意味）。しかし、一般的には、臆病者は良いものは何も手に入れることができない、の意。

「少し愛して、長く愛して」
（はげしい愛情は決して長続きしない）
「もし金の価値を知りたいなら、いくらか借りてみようとするがよい」
「ムチを惜しめば子供がダメになる」
　子供のことを本当に愛している両親は、必要な時に罰を与えることを怠ってはならない。罰を受けたことのない子供は、自分本位になってしまう。

— Every little
Makes a mickle (much great deal).

The Story of Alkestis.

There was in ancient Greece a King called Admetus, who was young and very wealthy. He had a very beautiful wife called Alkestis, and some children. But he became sick,— very sick. And the gods sent him word that he would die unless he could find some one else willing to die in his place.

Then the King made proclamation of what the gods had said, and made enquiry through all the land who was willing to die for him. But the people all said: "The light of the sun is sweet and death is dark & cold. And we do not want to die."

Then the King asked his father who was ninety-nine years old,— saying:— "O father, you have lived very long time and have enjoyed this world. But I am very young, and it is hard for me to die.

— Every little
      Makes a mickle (much great deal)

The Story of Alkestis.

  There was in ancient Greece a King called Admetus, who was young and very wealth*¹ He had a very beautiful wife called Alkestis, and some children. But he became sick, — very sick.　　And the Gods sent a word to him that he would die unless he could find some one*² else willing to die in his place.

  Then the King made proclamation of what the Gods had said, and made enquiry through all the land who was willing to die for him. But the people all said: "The light of the sun is sweet and death is dark & cold. And we do not want to die."

  Then the King asked his father who was ninety-nine years old, — saying: —"O father, you have lived very long time, and have enjoyed this world. But I am very young, and it is hard for me to die.

---

*1 wealthy
*2 someone

一塵も積もれば山となる

アルケスティスの物語

古代ギリシャにアドメトスという王がいた。王は若く、そして裕福であった。王にはアルケスティスというとても美しい王妃がおり、何人かの子供をもうけていた。しかし王は病気になった、たいへん重い病気になった。誰か進んで彼の身代わりとなって死んでくれる人間を見つけなければ、王はこのまま死んでしまうだろう、との神託が下された。
　そうして王は神託の内容を国民に知らせ誰か彼のために命を差し出すものがいないか国中にお触れを出した。しかし、人々は口をそろえて「日の光は心地よいが、死は暗く冷たい。死にたくはない。」と言った。

　次に王は九十九歳になる父親にたずねた「ああ、父上、あなたは十分に長生きをし、現世を楽しみました。しかし私はまだ若く、死ぬのは辛いのです。

Therefore, if you love me, you will die in my place."

But the old man became very angry and said:— "Son, I brought you into this world, and gave you this kingdom, and in all things did my duty to you. But it is not my duty to die for you. In this country it is the custom for sons to die for their fathers,— not for fathers to die for their sons. You are not a true son. You are not a true man. You are a coward,— a beast."

Then King Admetus became very angry with his father. But Alkestis, his wife, came and said,— "Do not speak unkindly to your father. I will die for you. Yet it be said that I must leave my little children. Be good to them when I am dead. And I will go and die."

Then Admetus was very sorry,— for he did not want to lose his young wife. But he was so afraid of death that he allowed her to die. So she died and her body was burned.

Then the old man, the father of Alkestis,

Therefore, if you love me, "you will die in my place."

But the old man became very angry and said; – "Son, I brought you into this world, and gave you this kingdom, and in all things did my duty to you. But it is not my duty to die for you. In this country it is the custom for sons to die for their fathers, — not for fathers to die for their sons. You are not a <u>true</u> son. You are not a true man. You are a coward — a beast."

Then King Admetus became very angry with his father. But Alkestis, his wife, came and said, — "Do not speak unkindly to your father. I will die for you. Yet it is sad that I *must* leave my little children. Be good to them, when I am dead. And I will go and die."

Then Admetus was very sorry, — for he did not want to lose his young wife. But he was so afraid of death that he allowed her to die. So he*¹ died and her body was <u>burned</u>.

Then the old man, the father of Alkestis*²

だから、もし私のことを愛しているのならば、私の身代わりに死んでください。

しかし、老人は激怒し、言った。「息子よ、私はお前をこの世界に産み落としてやり、そしてこの王国を与えた。親としてのお前に対する私の義務は、これで全てだ。お前のために死ぬことは私の義務ではない。この国には、息子は自らの父親のために命を差し出すという慣習はあれど、息子のために父親が命を差し出す、というものはない。お前はもう私の本当の息子ではない。人間でもない。この臆病もの―畜生め。」

するとアドメトス王は父親に激怒した。しかし、彼の妻、アルケスティスがやってきて言った。「お父様にそんな酷いことを言うものではありません。私があなたのために死にましょう。しかし、私の幼い子供達を置いていかなくてはいけないのは悲しいことです。私が死んだら、子供たちをよろしく頼みます。そうすれば、私は死にに行きましょう。」

アドメトスは非常にすまなく思った、彼は若い妻を失くしたくはなかったのだ。しかし彼は死ぬことがあまりにも恐ろしく、妻を死なせることにした。そうして、彼女は死に、遺体は燃やされた。

すると、アドメトスの老父は息子に言った。

---

*1 she のまちがいでは？
*2 Admetus のまちがいでは？

said to his son:— "Did I not speak the truth when I said you were a beast & a coward? You have allowed this woman to die for you. Even a woman is braver than you. And you have left your children without a mother. You are a murderer — you are a dog!"

And they quarrelled; and Admetus & his father separated; and all the people mourned for Alkestis.

But after a little time Admetus felt how cowardly and how selfish he had been, — and knew himself despised by all men, — and he locked himself up alone in his chamber and wept for Alkestis.

said to his son: — "Did I not speak the truth when I said you were a beast & a coward ? You have allowed this woman to die for you. Even a woman is braver than you. And you have left your children without a mother. You are a murderer — You are a dog !"

And they quarreled; and Admetus & his father separated; and all the people mourned for Alkestis.

But after a little time Admetus felt how cowardly and how selfish he had been, — and knew himself despised by all men, — and he locked himself up alone in his chamber and wept for Alketis*.

「お前が臆病者の畜生だと言ったのは、本当であったであろう？お前は自分のために、この女を死なせたのだ。女ですら、お前よりも勇敢なのだ。その上、お前は自らの子供の母親を奪ったのだ。お前は殺人者だ、—この犬畜生め！」

そして二人は言い争いをし、アドメトスと父親は決別した。国民全てがアルケスティスの死を悼んだ。

しかし、ほどなくしてアドメトスは自分がいかに臆病で身勝手であったかをさとり、またあらゆる人に自分が軽蔑されていること知ると、部屋に一人で籠り、アルケスティスのために涙を流したのであった。

---

* Alkestis

a coward — noun
cowardly — adjective (This, like lovely,
                        godly etc though
cowardice — abstract.   ending in LY is
cowardlily — adverb   not an adverb.)
           (are used)

timidity = natural fear or anxiety, not
        contemptible or wrong.
cowardice = blameworthy or disgraceful fear
        — selfish fear.

brute courage = the courage of an animal
        — without reason or care of
          consequence.
Pluck — manly courage.

Selfishness abstract.) abstract
                    Generosity
                      stronger
                    Self-sacrifice.

affection — for a friend, &c
love — " relative &c
filial love (of a son for his father
paternal — of a father for his son
maternal — mother
fraternal — brother.

A coward — noun
Cowardly — adjective (This, like lovely, godly etc. though ending in LY is not an adverb.)
Cowardice — abstract.
Cowardlily — rare used (adverb)

timidity = natural fear or anxiety, not contemptible or wrong.
Cowardice = blameworthy or disgraceful fear — selfish fear.

brute courage = the courage of an animal — without reason or care of consequence.
Pruck* — manly courage.
Selfishness   abstract | abstract
                        | Generosity
                        | stronger
                        | Self-sacrifice.

affection — for a friend, &c
love   —   〃 relative &c.
filial love   (of a son for his father
paternal — of a father for his son
maternal — mother
fraternal — brother

A coward（臆病者）— 名詞
Cowardly（臆病な）— 形容詞
　　　　（lyで終わっているが、この単語はlovely、godly などと同様に副詞ではない）
Cowardice（臆病）— 抽象概念
Cowardlily（おどおどして）— 副詞、あまり使われることは無い

timidity = 自然な恐怖や不安の感情で、軽蔑に値するものでも間違ったものでもない。
Cowardice = 非難に値する、不名誉な恐怖心。身勝手な恐怖心。

野蛮な勇気 — 動物のような勇気
　　　　　—理由がなく、結果に対する配慮が欠けている、
Pluck（度胸）— 男らしい勇気
Selfishness（身勝手さ） 抽象概念 | 抽象概念
                                | 寛大さ
                                | より強い
                                | 自己犠牲

affection（愛情）— 友達などに対する
love（愛情）— 親族に対する
filial   love   子どもの父に対する愛
paternal — 父の子に対する愛
maternal — 母の子に対する愛
fraternal — 兄弟に対する愛

---

* Pluck

Paper-money as a general term has no plural, — just like the words "gold", "silver". There is also a general term for metal money, COIN, (in business CASH) — but coin has also a plural form — coinS. This plural is generally used in relation to NUMISMATICS. — "The coins of Davis," "old Japanese coins," "A collector of coins." We cannot say "goldS" or "silverS" — but we say "copperS" — meaning copper coins.
"I gave him a few coppers."

To <u>cash</u> a bill = to change it into specie or coin.

Change (noun) = cash — or the money given back when a large bill has been cashed, — or small coin kept by a merchant for convenience.

If I wish to buy a book worth 4 yen, and I gave the merchant a 5-dollar bill, — I do not pay him that bill. I gave it him to change. After he has given me back 1 yen, he is paid,

Paper-money as a general term has no plural, — just like the words "gold," " silver"
　There is also a general term for metal money, COIN, (in business CASH) — but coin has also a plural form — coinS. This plural is generally used in relation to NUMISMATICS — "the coin<u>s</u> of Davis" "old Japanese coin<u>s</u>," "A collector of coins,"　We cannot say "golds" or silver<u>S</u> — but we say "copper<u>S</u>." — meaning Copper coins.

　　　　"I gave him a few copper<u>s</u>."
To <u>cash</u> a bill = to change it into specie or coin.
Change (noun) = cash — or the money given back when a large bill has been cashed, — or small coin kept by a merchant for convenience.

　If I wish to buy a book worth 4 yen, and I gave the merchant a 5-dollar bill, — I do not <u>pay</u> him that bill. I g^i ave it him to change. <u>After</u> he has given me back 1yen, he is <u>paid</u>,

一般用語としての Paper-money（紙幣）という語には複数形が無い。「金」や「銀」という単語も同じである。金属の貨幣を指す一般用語は COIN（硬貨）である。（商売の際は CASH）だが COIN（硬貨）には複数形があり、coinS になる。この複数形は NUMISMATICS（貨幣の研究）で用いられる。—「デイビス硬貨」「日本の古い硬貨」「コインの収集家」金や銀を複数形で言うことはできないが、銅は複数形 "copperS" になり、銅貨を意味する。

　　　「私は彼に銅貨数枚をあげた。」
紙幣を小銭に換える　—　お札を正貨や硬貨に変えること
Change（名詞）くずした金　—　現金—または大きい額面の紙幣を受けとった時に返す釣銭
　　　　—　もしくは、商売人が便宜上手元においておく少額の硬貨

もし私が四円相当の本を買おうと思い、店員に五ドル札を渡した—とする—、私はその紙幣分 "pay"（支払う）のではない。私は店員にお釣りをもらうためにそのお札を渡した。店員から１円のお釣りをもらってはじめて、代金が店員に "paid"（支払われた）ことになる。

not before.

"The price was four dollars; so I handed (gave) the merchant a five-dollar bill; and he gave me back 1 dollar change.

Store-idioms
Merchant, (receiving a 20-dollar bill) "Cash!"
Boy runs up, takes the bill and goes with it to the cashier.
Customer: — "I have very little time, — please hurry with that change."
Boy, (returning) "Here is your change, sir."

The verb to CASH is also used of cheques, drafts, money-orders, etc. —
"To cash a cheque"
"To cash a money-order"
"To cash a draft"
"To change a bill."

not before.
"The price was four dollar*¹, so I handed (gave) the merchant a five-doller*² bill; and he gave me back 1 doller*³ change.

その前ではない。
「代金は四ドルだったので、私は店員に五ドル札を渡しました。そして彼は一ドルのお釣りを返しました。」

Store-idioms
Merchant (receiving a 20-dollar bill)
"Cash !"
　Boys runs up, takes the bill and goes with it to the casher.
　Customer: — "I have very little time, — please hurry with that change."
　Boy（returning）"Here is your change, sir!"
The verb to CASH is also used of cheques drafts, money-order, etc.
　　"To cash a cheque"
　　"To cash a money-order"
　　"To cash a draft"
　　　　To change a bill.

店で使う慣用表現
店主（二十ドル札を受け取る）
「お釣り！」
丁稚が走り寄り、
その紙幣を受け取ってレジ台に向かう。
客：―「時間がほとんどないんです、急いでお釣りをください。」
丁稚（戻ってきて）「こちらがお釣りです！」

CASHという動詞は、
小切手や為替手形や郵便為替などでも使われる
「小切手を現金に換える」
「為替を現金に換える」
「為替手形を現金に換える」
「紙幣を小銭に換える」

---

*1 dollars
*2 dollar
*3 dollar

Post office.

The Kumamoto P.O. sends letters to Tokyo, and delivers letters in Kumamoto.

All letters, books, papers, — everything which passes through the P.O. — is called with by one word, — Mail. — "from a Celtic word meaning bag."

The man who delivers the mail is called postman or mail-carrier.

A train which carries mail is called a Mail-train.

A steamer " " a mail-steamer.

The mail addressed to any place is called by the name of the place from which or to which, it is sent.

"The Kyūshū mail was delivered in Tokyo on Saturday."

"The Tokyo mail is expected here this evening."

"The American mail is due at Yokohama on the 31st."

Post office
The Kumamoto P.O sends letters to Tokyo, and delivers letters in Kumamoto. All letters, books, papers, — everything which passes through a P.O – is called ~~with~~ by one word, — Mail. Mailer
"from a Celtic word meaning bag."
The man who delivers the mail is called postman or mail-carrier.

A train which carries mail is called a Mail-train
A steamer 〃　〃* a mail steamer

The mail addressed to any place is called by the name of the place from which or to which, it is sent.
"The Kyushu mail was delivered in Tokyo on Saturday."
"The Tokyo mail is expected here this evening."
"The American mail is due at Yokohama on the 31 st."

郵便局
熊本郵便局は手紙を東京に送り、熊本で手紙を配達する。全ての手紙や、本、新聞、郵便局を通過するものは全て Mail という一語で呼ばれる。Mailer
「袋」を意味するケルト語が由来である。

郵便物を配達する人は
postman もしくは mail-carrier と呼ばれる。

郵便物を運ぶ列車は Mail-train と呼ばれる。
蒸気船の場合は、Mail steamer と呼ばれる。

どこに宛てた郵便物でも、
投函元と行き先の場所の名前で呼ばれる。

「九州からの郵便物が
土曜日に東京で配達された。」
「東京からの郵便物は
今夜着くはずだ。」
「アメリカからの郵便物が
三十一日に横浜に届くことになっている。」

* is called の意味

"The Hong-Kong mail closes on Tuesday at 10 a.m."

Letters containing money are REGISTERED for safety.

"I wish to have this letter registered."

"You must always sign a receipt for a registered letter."

from RE? a thing. ETERERE to bring events hence a record of

"The Hong-Kong mail closes on Tuesday at 10 a.m."
 Letters containing money are REGISTERED for safety.
   "I wish to have this letter Registered."
   "You must always sign a receipt for a registered letter.
from RES a thing. GERERE to bring ［events Hence a record of

「香港への郵便は火曜日の十時に締め切られる。」
現金を含む手紙は安全のため REGISTERED（書留）にされる。
「この手紙を書留にしたいのですが。」
「書留の手紙の場合、かならず受領書にサインをしなくてはいけない。」
ラテン語の RES は物。GERERE 運ぶ。したがって、物事の記録、という意味である。

The 3rd Term.

Few idioms in travelling by train.

TO TAKE (a) train —

Trains are distinguished and named according to the hours at which they start or arrive.

ex. — "I wish to take the 5 o'clock train for Hakata today."

My friend left Moji this morning by the 4 o'clock train. I expect him (by) the 11.30 train.

"The train FOR —— (name of place to which it is going)
He will take the train for Kumamoto today.

To <u>take</u> a steamer, or carriage, boat.
 "   "   a house ——→ sense of "occupy."

Proverbs.

Diamond cut diamond.
(Refers to character. A dangerous or cunning man can only be encountered by another as hard as himself.)

The 3rd Term.
few idioms in traveling by train.
TO TAKE {a / the} train —
Trains are distinguished and named according to the hours at which they start or arrive.

EX. — "I wish to take the 5 o'clock train for Hakata today."

My friend left Moji this morning by the 4 o'clock train. I expect him {by / on} the 11:30 train.

"The train FOR — (name of place to which it is going)

He will take the (---) train for Kumamoto today.

To take a steamer, or carriage, boat,
　〃　〃　a house ——— sense of "occupy."

Proverbs
Diamond cut diamond.
　(Refers to character. A dangerous or cunning man can only be encountered by another as hard as himself.)

3学期
汽車での旅に関する慣用句
To Take {a / the} train （汽車に乗る）
　　　　　　　　　　　（その汽車に乗る）

汽車は出発時刻、もしくは到着時刻によって区別され呼ばれる。

例.「今日の五時の博多行きの汽車に乗りたいのですが。」
私の友人は今朝4時の汽車で門司を発った。11時半到着予定の電車で来ると私は思っている。

The train FOR—（行き先の名前）

彼は今日（〜時発の）熊本行きの汽車に乗る。

蒸気船に乗る、馬車に乗る、ボートに乗る、家を借りる、このtakeには「占有する」という意味がある

諺
金剛石を削るには金剛石を持ってせよ
（性格に関して言う。危険な、または、ずる賢い人間には、それと同じくらい無情な人間でないと対抗できない。）

Set a thief to catch a thief — is a
  limited form of the same proverb.

Don't drive a second nail until the
  first is CLINCHED.
   (Never begin a new enterprise until
   you are perfectly sure of having finished the old. Never have an undertaking half finished, in order to begin another.)

Fortune favours the bold.
Look before you leap.
The dog wags his tail, not for you, but
  for the bread.
Dogs that bark at a distance never bite.
   (Men who threaten us behind our
   backs never have courage to do us
   any harm when we are present.)

There are many ways of killing a
  dog without chocking him with butter.
   (One should always consider the cheapest
   & the best way of doing things.)

Set a thief to catch a thief — is a
 limbed*¹ form of the same proverb.

Don't drive a second nail until the
 first is CLINCHED.
(Never begin a new enterprise until
 you are perfectly sure of having finished the old . Never leave an undertaking half finished, in order to begin another.)

Fortune favours the bold.
Look before you leap.
The dog wags his tail, not for you, but
 for the bread.
Dogs that bark at a distance never bite.
(Men who threaten us behind our
 backs never have courage to do us
any harm when we are present.)

There are many ways of killing a
 dog without chocking*² him with butter.
(One should always consider the cheapest
 & the best way of doing things.)

盗人を捕まえるには盗人をもってせよ（蛇の道は蛇）―同じ諺だが意味が狭い

最初の釘がしっかり打ち付けられるまで、二本目の釘に手を出すな。
（前のものを確実に終わらせるまで、新しい企てを起こすな。 新しいものを始めるために、いったん始めた企てを中途半端にしておくな。）

運命の女神は勇敢な者に味方する。
跳ぶ前に見よ（転ばぬ先の杖）
犬がしっぽを振るのは、あなたに対してではなく、エサに対してである。
遠くで吼えている犬は、決して噛みついてこない。
（私達の背後で脅してくるような人間は、私達が目前にいる時は私達に危害を加える勇気は無い。）

バターで窒息させなくとも、
犬を殺す方法はいくらでもある。
（人は何かをするうえで、常に最も安上がりで最善の方法を模索するべきだ。）

---

*1 limited か
*2 choking

Better a blush in the face than a spot in the heart.
It is better to confess that one is in the wrong, than to keep a bad conscience.

Sounds.
Sounds are loud or low.*

{Strong, great} — or {weak, faint, feeble}

* This word low has two entirely opposite meanings.

Low sounds of immense power are called by a particular adjective — DEEP

A clap of thunder — the roar of surf in a storm, — wind in pines. — the sound of cannon, — a great bell's tolling — are deep.

Sounds which are very high and also very powerful are called SHRILL.
(The steam whistle of train is shrill.)

Better a blush in the face than a spot in the heart.
(It is better to confess that one is in the wrong, than to keep a bad conscience.

Sounds

Sounds are loud or low ※

$\begin{Bmatrix} \text{Strong} \\ \text{Great} \end{Bmatrix}$ — or $\begin{Bmatrix} \text{weak} \\ \text{faint} \\ \text{feeble} \end{Bmatrix}$

※ This word low has two entirely opposite meanings.

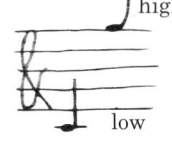

♩ high
low

Low sounds of immense power are called by a particular adjective — DEEP

A clap of thunder — the roar of surf in a storm, — wind in pines, — the sound of cannon, — a great bell's tolling — are <u>deep</u>.

Sounds which are very high and also very powerful are called

SHRILL.

(The Steam whistle of train is shrill.)

心に汚点があるよりも、顔を赤らめるほうが良い。
（心にやましいことを抱えているよりも、自分が悪かったと告白した方が良い）

音

音は、大きいか、低い ※

$\begin{Bmatrix} \text{強い} \\ \text{大きい} \end{Bmatrix}$ または $\begin{Bmatrix} \text{弱い} \\ \text{かすかな} \\ \text{微弱な} \end{Bmatrix}$

※この low という語は全く正反対の二つの意味を持つ

♩ 高い
低い

力強くて低い音は、特別の形容詞―DEEP―と呼ばれる
雷鳴のゴロゴロという音
嵐の時の打ち寄せる波の轟音
松が風に揺れる音
大砲の音
大きな鐘が鳴る音―は deep である。

甲高く力強い音は―SHRILL―と呼ばれる。
（列車の汽笛は shrill である）

Among them there are the sound of a steam-whistle, — the sounds made by semi in summer, — the voices of children at play (sometimes), — the cry of certain birds, such as the kite.

Tennyson uses the verb "to shrill" in speaking of a woman's voice. "She shrilled to him" — instead of "she cried out to him." But this is only lawful in poetry. In prose we could not use it.

All these sounds may be agreeable or disagreeable.

The word <u>sweet</u> is used to qualify

SOUND — "The sweet sound of a flute —
            The sweet coo of a dove."
TASTE —
  SMELL —
    CHARACTER — "This child has a sweet disposition."
      ASPECT — "The old mother had a sweet face."

'Tis sweet to hear the watchdog's honest bark
  Bay deep-mouthed welcome as we draw near home;
'Tis sweet to know there is an eye will mark
  Our coming, & look brighter when we come.
                  — Byron.

    Among ^them there are the sound of a steam-
    whistle — the sounds made by <u>semi</u>
    in summer, — the voices of children
    at play (sometimes), — the cry of certain
    birds, such as the kite.
Tennyson uses the verb "to shrill" in
 speaking of a woman's voice.
 "She <u>shrilled</u> to him" —　instead of "she
 cried out to him." But this is only
 lawful in poetry. In prose we could
 not use it.

All these sounds may be agr^ee able or
disagreeable.
    The word sweet is used to qualify
SOUND　— The <u>sweet</u> sound of a flute.
          The sweet coo of a dove.
   TASTE　—
     SMELL　—
       CHARACTER　— This child has a
                   sweet disposition.
        ASPECT　　"The old mother
                   had a sweet face.

'Tis <u>sweet</u> to hear the watch dog's honest bark
  Bay deep-mouthed welcome as we draw near home,
'Tis sweet to know there is an eye wilt mark
  Our coming, & look brighter when we come
                        — Byron.

shrillという音には、蒸気機関車の汽笛の音
―夏の蝉の声
―子供が遊ぶ声（時々）
―ある種の鳥、鳶などの鳴き声
などがある。
テニスンは"to shrill"（甲高い声で話す）という動詞を女性の声について述べる時に用いる。
「彼女は彼に金切り声をあげた」―
「彼女は彼に叫んだ」と言う代わりに。
しかしこれは詩作にのみ認められた使用法である。散文では、これは使えないだろう。

これらの音は好ましいものにも、不愉快なものにもなりうる。
sweetという語は（以下のものを）修飾する際に使われる
音―フルートの心地よい音色
   鳩のクークーという可愛らしい鳴き声
味―
   匂い―
     性格―この子供は可愛らしい性格をしている
     顔つき―年老いた母親は優しい顔をしていた

「家に近づくとき、忠実な番犬が喜び迎えて吠える、
　低い太い唸り声を聞くのは愉しいものである。」
「われらの来るのを見守って、われらの帰りついたとき、
　輝きをます目があると知るのは愉しいものである。」
　　　　　　　　　　　　　―バイロン[6]

---

[6] バイロン『ドン・ジュアン　上』小川和夫訳、冨山房、1993年。(canto Ⅰ, cxxⅲ)

85

Adjectives expressing roughness, unevenness, are also used to qualify sounds — "harsh," "rude," "broken," "irregular."
Adjectives expressing sharpness, or cutting power are also used to qualify certain painful sounds — "keen," "sharp" — "piercing," — "penetrating," — &c.

All such terms as melodious, harmonious, musical, &c — are, strictly speaking, not to be used often. For they refer to music — not to sound pure & simple.

All uses of "harmony" or "harmonious" must simply mean multiplicity of sounds in combination.

"Melody" or "melodious" may refer, on the contrary, to a single tone, — but with a musical suggestion.

Sights.
  A "sight" is "a seeing" — and by transference the thing seen. Spectacle has almost exactly the same meaning and can be used in exactly the same way.

Adjectives expressing roughness, unevenness, are also used to qualify sounds —
 "harsh," "rude," "broken," "irregular."

Adjectives expressing sharpness, or cutting power are also used to qualify certain painful sounds, — "keen," — "sharp" "piercing," — "penetrating," — etc.
All such terms as melodious, harmonious, musical, etc. are, strictly speaking, not to be used often. For they refer to music — not to sound pure & simple.
　All uses of "harmony" or "harmonious" must simply multiplicity of sounds in combination.
"Melody" or "melodious" may refer, on the contrary, to a single tone, — but with a musical suggestion.

<u>Sights</u>
　"A sight" is "a seeing" — and by transference <u>the thing seen</u>. Spectacle has almost exactly the same meaning and can be used in exactly the same way.

粗さやムラを表す形容詞もまた、音を形容するのに用いられる—
「耳障りな」「粗雑な」「途切れ途切れ」「不規則な」など

鋭さや切り刻む力を表す形容詞もまたある種の耳を掩いたくなるような音を表すのに用いられる。—「鋭い」—「とがった」—「つんざくような」—「つきやぶるような」—などなど

豊かな旋律の、調和のとれた、音楽的な、などこれらの語は、厳密にいうと、そう頻繁に使われるべきものではない。なぜならこれらの語は音楽に対して用いられるものであり、ただの純然たる音には用いられないものだからである。
　"harmony"や"harmonious"という語を用いる場合は必ず音が組み合わさって多層的になっていなければならない。
　一方、"melody"や"melodious"は、単音であってもいいが音楽性を示唆するものである。

Sights（見ること）
　"A sight"とは「見ること」である—またそこから転じて、<u>見られているもの</u>でもある。Spectacle（光景）という語はほぼ全く同義であり、全く同様に用いることが可能である。

spectacle.
(1). The sight of a plum tree in full bloom is beautiful.   [sight! (spectacle)
(2). A plum tree in full bloom is a beautiful _____ in apposition.

The same idea can be expressed in 3 common ways:
I. A cherry tree in bloom is a beautiful sight.
II. The sight of a cherry tree in bloom is beautiful.
III. A cherry tree in bloom is beautiful TO SEE.

     Subject   adj.
"A field of a battle"   "awful"
I. The sight of a field of battle is awful.
II. A field of a battle is an awful sight.
III. " " " " " is awful to see.

    Much more difficult and complicated is the use of the word VIEW. This word has a much more limited meaning and is very seldom a synonym for sight or spectacle. Anything seen may be called "a sight." But only a certain particular class of things can be called VIEWS.
    Yet view has only 3 meanings:

(spectacle)
(1) The sight of a plum tree in full bloom is
       beautiful.   [sight. (spectacle)
(2) A plum tree in full bloom is a beautiful
       in apposition.
The same idea can be expressed in 3 common ways.

Ⅰ A cherry tree in bloom is a beautiful sight.
Ⅱ The sight of a cherry tree in bloom is beautiful.
Ⅲ A cherry tree in bloom is beautiful TO SEE.

   Subject   Adj.
 "A field of a battle" "awful"
Ⅰ The sight of a field of battle is awful.
Ⅱ A field of a battle is an awful sight
Ⅲ 〃   〃   〃   〃 is awful to see.

  Much more difficult and complicated
is the use of the word VIEW. This word has
a much more limited mean*, and is very
seldom a synonym for sight or spectacle.
Anything seen may be called a "sight."
But only a certain particular class of things,
can be called VIEWS.
 Yet view has only 3 meanings.

(1) 満開の梅の木の景色は美しい。

(2) 満開の梅の木は、美しい光景である。
          同格である
同じ発想は三通りの言い方で表現することができる。
Ⅰ 桜の花が咲いているのは、美しい光景だ
Ⅱ 桜の花が咲いている光景は、美しい
Ⅲ 桜の花が咲いているのは、眺めて美しい。

   主語   形容詞
「戦場」   「恐ろしい」
Ⅰ 戦場の光景は恐ろしい
Ⅱ 戦場は恐ろしい光景だ
Ⅲ 戦場は見るだに恐ろしい

はるかに難しく複雑であるのがVIEWという単語の使用である。この語にはるかに制限された意味しかなく、SightやSpectacleと同義であることはほとんどない。
どんなものでも"sight"と言えるが、ある特別な部類のものしかVIEWSと呼ぶことができない。
そのviewには３通りの意味しかない。

---

*meaning

uses of picture

I. — A landscape, or large scene.

II. — A picture (photograph or painting of a landscape or large scene)

III. — A synonym for "look" or "sight" in an idiomatic phrase.

The idiom in question is "to take a look at", "to get a look at."

"I took a look at the house," (i.e. I looked at
 I get a good look at the man (i.e. I saw the house
 able to see the man)

Now the word <u>view</u>, followed by the preposition "of" is frequently substituted for "look at" in these idioms.

"I went to the theatre, but I could not get a good (view of / look at) the stage."

"I got a good view of his face."

In such cases the meaning of <u>view</u> is simply <u>look</u> or <u>sight</u>.

"I have a book called VIEWS of LONDON." (i.e. A book of pictures of London — large scenes of streets, &c.

items of picture
- I — A landscape, or large scene.
- II — A picture photograph or painting of a landscape or large scene)
- III — A synonym for "look" or "sight" in an idiomatic phrase.

The idiom in question is "to take a look at" "to get a look at"

"I took a look at the house," (i.e. I looked at the house.)

"I got a good look at the man. (i.e. I was able to see the man.)

Now the word <u>view</u>, followed by the preposition "of" is frequently substituted for "look at" in these idioms.

"I went to the theatre, but I could not get a good (view of / look at) the stage.

"I got a good view of his face."

In such cases the meaning of <u>view</u> is simply <u>look</u> or <u>sight</u>.

I have a book called VIEWS of LONDON.
(i.e. A book of pictures of London — large scenes of streets, &c.

画像の類
- I — 風景、もしくは広大な景色
- II — 風景や広大な景色の写真や絵画
- III — 慣用表現においては "look" や "sight" と同義になる

問題の慣用句とは "to take a look at" "to get a look at" である。

「私は家を見てみた」(つまり、私は家を見た、ということ)

「私はその男性をしげしげと眺めた」
(つまり、その男性をよく見ることができた、ということ)

view という語は、前置詞の "of" を後ろにつけると、しばしば以下のような慣用表現において "look at" の代わりに用いられる。

「劇場に行ったが、舞台をよく見ることができなかった。」
「彼の顔をしげしげと眺めた。」
これらの場合では view という語の意味は単に look や sight ということである。

私は VIEWS of LONDON（ロンドンの景色）という本を持っている。
　(すなわち、街路などの広い光景などが写っている、ロンドンの街の写真の本)

VIEWS of TOKYO | SIGHTS of TOKYO.
(or) Pictures of Tokyo | Theatres, Gardens, the curiosities, the things everybody goes to see

By another process of transference (symbolical) the word *view* has come to be used as an equivalent for "opinion." The history of this is curious. It is shown in our idiom:— "From such a point of view." *A point of view* really meant a high place from which we can see a great space.

In such a case view becomes a synonym of opinion. "What are your views?" (What are your opinions.) — anciently meaning "How do you see this?"

Every-day we read in the Japanese newspaper about "the views of the Minister," "the views of the Parliament." It is a more polite and a much larger word than *opinion*, — though synonymous.

	— kenbutsu
VIEWS of Tokyo	SIGHTS of Tokyo.
i.e. Pictures of Tokyo	the theaters, the gardens, the curiosities, the things every-body goes to see

 By another process of transference, symbolical)   the word view has come to be used as an equivalent for "opinion." "The history of this is obvious. It is shown in our idiom: — From such a point of view. A point of view really meant a high place from which we can see a great space.

  In such a case view becomes a synonym of opinion. "What are your views?" (What are your opinions? — anciently meaning "How do you see this?"

  Every-day we read in the Japanese newspaper about "the views of the Minister." "the views of the Parliament. It is a more polite and a much large word than opinion, — though synonymous.

	— 見物
東京の景色	東京の見所
東京の絵	劇場、庭園、珍しいもの、事物など 万人が見に行くもの

また言葉の意味が転じることによって、象徴的に view という語は "opinion" の同義語として使われるようになった。この経緯は明らかであり、我々の慣用句—そのような観点からみると—に表れている。A point of view とは元来見晴らしの良い高台を指していた。

　このような場合、view は opinion の同義語である。
「あなたの見解は何ですか？」
（あなたの意見は何ですか？—古くは「どのようにご覧になりますか？」という意味）

　毎日我々は日本の新聞で「大臣の見解」「議会の見解」について読んでいる。これは opinion の同義語ではあるが、それよりも丁寧な語で、より広い意味を持つ。

"Composition".

1. About Fun.

Fun = that sort of pleasure which causes laughter, excitement, and shouting — generally of an amiable kind.

For instance, playing cards is only an amusement — not fun. But if the rule of the game is that the loser must have his face blackened, then there is a great deal of fun.

A funny story, a story that makes everybody laugh.

"Fun" is an abstract noun.

Jest — something funny spoken.

Joke — something funny either done or spoken.

Fun — Anything which causes happy excitement and laughter.

If your friend becomes angry while playing, you use the apologetic expression :—
"Don't be vexed — it was only fun" — or "only for fun".

Jokes which are acted not spoken, are called

Composition

1. About Fun.

fun = that sort of pleasure which causes laughter, excitement, and shouting — generally of an amiable kind.

For instance, playing cards is only an amusement — not fun. But of* the rule of the game is that the loser must have his face blackened then there is a great deal of fun.

   A funny story, a story that makes everybody laugh.

"Fun" is an abstract noun.

  Jest — something funny <u>spoken</u>

  Joke — something funny either <u>done</u> or <u>spoken</u>.

  Fun — Anything which causes happy excitement and laughter.

   If your friend becomes angry while playing, you use the apologetic expression: —
  "Don't be vexed": — "it was only fun" — or "only for fun"

  Jokes which are <u>acted</u> not spoken, are called

---

* if

practical joke.
A Jest — may be either evil or harmless.
A cruel fun
 Jest at the expense of another persons constitute
what is called "ridicule."
Irony — speaking to a person in terms of ex-
    aggerated praise or admiration in order to
    make him feel ashamed or angry.
Satire — is generally used only of _written_ ridicule.
    It is not _veiled_ like irony, but frankly
    hostile.
Fun always gives the idea of harmless, amiable
    pleasure. The ridicule of irony or satire may
    cause us to laugh; but it is not fun.
Entertainment (a larger word than amusement)
    generally refers to some form of pleasure prepar-
    ed for the enjoyment of many persons.
        Ex. "A banquet" or a performance in a
            theatre" &c.

2.

BY him — (always refers properly to the person
    acting — therefore the DIRECT instrument.)
THROUGH him — (always refers to the person assisting
    or helping the action — therefore the INDIRECT

practical joke.
A Jest — may be either evil or harmless.
A cruel fun
Jest at the expense of another*1 persons constitute*2 what is called "ridicule".

irony — speaking to a person in terms of exaggerated prase or admiration in order to make him feel ashamed or angry.
Satire — is generally used only of written ridicule.
It is not veiled like irony, but frankly hostile.

fun always gives the idea of harmless, amiable pleasure. The ridicule of irony or satire may case us to laugh; but it is not fun.

Entertainment (a larger word than amusement) generally refers to some form of pleasure prepared for the enjoyment of many persons.
Ex. 'A banquet" or a performance in a theatre." etc.

2.
BY him — (always refers properly to the person acting — therefore the DIRECT instrument.)
THROUGH him — (always refers to the person assisting or helping the action — therefore the INDIRECT

practical joke（悪ふざけ）と呼ばれる。
A Jest（冗談）— 悪意のあるものも、害のないものも、どちらでもありうる残酷な笑い
他人をこけにする冗談は「嘲笑」と呼ばれるものとなる。
irony（皮肉）— 相手を恥ずかしく思わせたり怒らせたりするために、過度に褒めたり賞賛の言葉をかけたりすること
Satire（皮肉・風刺）— 一般的には書かれた嘲笑にのみ用いる。
ironyのように隠されたものではなく、あからさまに敵意のあるものである。
funは常に害がなく、好意的な喜びがあることを示す。皮肉や風刺によって生まれる嘲笑は我々を笑わせはするが、楽しいものではない。

娯楽 entertainment（amusementよりも広い語）は一般的には、多くの人が楽しめるように準備された娯楽のことを言う。
例．宴会や劇場での公演など

2．
BY him（彼によって）—（常に行動している人物その人を指す―したがって、直接的な動作主である。）
THROUGH him（彼のおかげで）—（常にその行動の補助をし、手助けをする人物を指す―したがって、間接的な動作主である。）

---

*1 other
*2 constitues

instrument.
(ex. "The work was done BY him." he himself did the work.)
"The work was done THROUGH him." (It was done by means of his assistance only.)

The word "Sea" in English refers only to a space of water bounded on three sides by land — larger than a gulf. There are a very few exceptions; but this is the rule. Instead of such expression as "the Sea of ———" we may say "the ——— COAST." According to English geography there is the Inland Sea, and the Sea of Japan.

(GULF) A sea space within the opening of the coast of one country, is not called a sea, but according to size, a Gulf or Bay.

No preposition is used after "appoint" in many cases where the office-title, follows the verb. "He was appointed {general, president, chief, headman}."
When the office is indicated by another word than the title, the construction is with a preposition. "He was appointed to the post of commander-in-chief." "He was appointed to the Presidency of Madras."

instrument.
 Ex. "The work was done BY him." (he himself did the work.)
  "The work was done THROUGH him" (It was done by means of his assistance only.)

The word "Sea" in English refers only to a space of water bounded on three sides by land — longer than a gulf. There are a very few exception*1 : but this in*2 the rule. Instead of such expression as "the Sea of ── " we may say "the ── COAST." According to English geography there is the Inland Sea and the Sea of Japan.

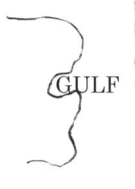

GULF { A sea space within the opening of the coast of one country, is not called a sea, but according to size, a Gulf or Bay.

No preposition is used after appoint in many cases where the office-terrie follows the verb.
 "He was appointed { general, president, chief, headman.

When the office is indicated by another word than the title, the construction is with a preposition.
 "He was appointed <u>to the post</u> of commander-in-chief.
 "He was appointed to the PresidenCY of Madras."

例.「この仕事は彼によってなされた」
 （彼自身がその仕事をした）
 「この仕事は彼のおかげでなされた」
 （彼の助力によってその仕事はなされた）

英語の Sea（海）というのは、三面が陸地に隣接している水の空間のみを指し、一gulf（湾）よりは長いものである。例外はきわめてわずかながらあるが、これが原則である。「一海」というような表現の代わりに、「一沿岸」と言うことがある。イギリスの地誌の本によると、内海（瀬戸内海）と日本海がある。

GULF { 一つの国の海岸の開口部にある海水の空間は、海ではなく、その大きさに従って Gulf（湾）や Bay（入江）と呼ばれる。

Appoint（任命する）という動詞の後に役職が続く場合には後ろに前置詞をつけないことが多い。
「彼は軍司令官、大統領、長官、村長に任命された。」
地位が、役職ではなく別の言葉で述べられるときは、文の構造には前置詞が用いられる。
「彼は総司令官の職に任ぜられた。」
「彼はマドラスの総督の職に任命された。」

---

*1 exceptions
*2 is

allegiance — the faithfulness, or the adhesion of a
   person or persons to a ruler or cause.
   (Special). "His allegiance to the King lasted
      10 years."
loyalty — abstract noun — a virtue. (General).
   "His loyalty to the King has made him
      famous."

from the bottom of the heart.
from the heart of the heart.

lower than an animal,   or
more shameless than an animal.

"to assault," — (to attack) requires the mention of
   the object or person attacked.
"to make an assault," — may be used without
   such mention.
ex. "Tonight the enemy will make an assault."
                          [meaning 夜襲をなすだろう
   Literary idiom ————————— 明日サムラフ可し Special
      "On the pinnacle of Fame."
A pinnacle is an architectural structure, — peculiar
to gothic architecture.

allegiance — the faithfulness, or the adhesion of a
    person or persons to a ruler or cause
    (Special). "His allegiance to the king lasted
    5 years."
loyalty — abstract noun — A virtue. (general).
    "His loyalty to the king has mad* him
    famous."

from the bottom of the heart
from the heart of the heart.

lower than an animal,   or
more shameless than an animal.

"to assault," — (to attack) requires the mention of
    <u>the object</u> or person attacked.

"to make an assault," — may be used without
    such mention.
    EX. " Tonight the enemy will make an assault."
                    〔meaning ヲ有スルコトアレバ也
<u>Literary idiom.</u> …… 用ヰサルヲ可トス   Special

    On the pinnacle of Fame
 A pinnacle is an architectural structure, — peculiar
to gothic architectures.

---
* made

allegiance（忠誠） ― 人や支配者、主義に対する忠実、忠誠 （特定のもの）
「彼の王に対する忠誠は５年間続いた。」
loyalty（忠誠） ― 抽象的な名詞 ― 美徳 （一般的なもの）
「彼は王への忠誠心で有名になった。」

心のそこから
心の内奥から

動物よりも劣る、もしくは
動物よりも恥知らず

"to assault"（襲撃する） ― （攻撃する）攻撃された物体や人物を言及する必要がある
"to make an assault"（襲撃する） ― そのような言及はなしで使うこともある
例．今夜敵が襲撃してくるだろう。

文語的な慣用句 …用いざるを可とす、特別な意味を有することがある
  名声の頂点
a pinnacle とは建造構造の一つであり、―ゴシック建築に特有のものである、

Pinnacle of trust. This phrase really means on the pinnacle [of the temple] of the goddess Fame.

Therefore the expression can only be used of an individual, or some one thing relating to an individual.

Always put the word OF between a date and the name of the month or period.
On the 5th of November.
In the 15th year of Meiji.

The simplicity of his ~~life~~
food, clothing, shelter, wants and customs, &c.

Provisions (1) a measure provided by law — a legal provision — a conditional law.
Provisions — food, supplies.

TO SHAME — to make a person feel ashamed
TO BE ASHAMED (of).
TO BE SHAMED (by).

Pinnacle of turret — This phrase really means on the pinnacle [of the temple] of [the Goddess Fame.

Therefore the expression can only be used of an individual or some one thing relating to an individual.

Always put the word OF between a date and the name of the month or period.
On the 5th of November.
In the 15th year of Meiji.

The simplicity of his life
    food, clothing, shelter, wants and customs, etc.
Provisions (1) a measure provided by law — a legal provision — a conditional law.
ProvisionS — food, supplies.
TO SHAME — to make a person feel ashamed
TO BE ASHAMED (of).
TO BE SHAMED (by).

小塔 "turret" の尖塔 "pinnacle" ── この語句は、実際は名声の女神を祀った寺院の尖塔の上を意味する。

したがって、この表現は個人か、個人に関するものにのみ用いられる。

日付と月や時代の間には常に OF を入れる。
十一月五日に
明治十五年に

無駄なものを省いた彼の生活
    食べ物、衣服、住居、必要な物、そして慣習などをいう
条例 provision（単数）── 法によって定められた決まり
    ── 法的な規定 ── 条件的な
食糧 provisions ── 食べ物、食糧品
辱める ── 人を恥ずかしい気持ちにさせる
〜を恥ずかしく思う
〜に辱められる

& pith splashes.

Everything that happens in the world {ought to / should} teach us — duty.

Loyalist — a term invented to designate a man faithful to the king's cause in time of Revolution. Therefore a special political name — not properly a common noun. The Royalists of the 17th century were the Cavaliers.

bk = a l .. The Forty-seven Loyal Retainers + 47

Learn of = to hear of, to get news of
Learn = to require perfect knowledge of — fully estimate.

Difference between Food & Provisions.
   food — nourishment.
   provisions — food stored for future's use.

~~Action is manifested~~
   Square tower and round tower
The buildings of a castle consist of towers and walls, — and a few other buildings inside the walls.

A fish splashes.

Everything that happens in the world $\begin{Bmatrix} \text{ought to} \\ \text{should} \end{Bmatrix}$ teach us — duty.

Loyalist — a term invented to designate a man faithful to the king's cause in time of Revolution. Therefore a special political name — not properly a common noun.   The Royalists of the 17th century were the Cavaliers.
  故ニ吾人ハ The Forty-seven Loyal Retainers ト イフ

Learn of = to hear of, to get news of NEWS
Learn = to acquire perfect knowledge of — fully estimate.

Difference between Food & Provisions.
 food — nourishment
 provisions — food stored for future's use.

Action is manifested.
  Square tower and ground*¹ tower
 The buildings of a castle consist of towers and walls, — and a few other buildings in-side*² the walls.

魚が跳ねる

この世界で起こる全てのことは我々に義務ということを教えている｜はず｜だ
        ｜べき｜

王党派 loyalist ― 革命の時に王を忠実に支持した人を呼ぶために作られた言葉。したがって特別な政治的な名称であって、一般的な普通名詞ではない。十七世紀の王党員 Royalists は the Cavaliers と呼ばれた。
 故に、赤穂浪士は The Forty-seven Loyal Retainers と呼ばれる

Learn of ＝　～について聞く、～について
     知る
Learn ＝　～について完全な知識を得る
   ―充分に判断する
Food と Provisions の違い
food　―　食べ物
provisions　―　将来のために蓄えられている食べ物

行動が示される
四角い塔と、円塔
城は塔と壁から成り立っている
―城壁の中にも他に二、三建物がある

---

*1 round
*2 inside

'to enshrine in —' to put into a shrine.
'to devise' = to plan, arrange, or to invent.

The place where a town stands (or stood) is called the SITE (the situation).

to play music — to use an instrument in making music.

to moo
to ~~get~~ low } of cattles.

to have
to get } a good appetite.
to feel

to have a taste (of ~~person~~ thing) — to have qualities which affect the nerves of the tongue.

to have a taste (of person) — to have some æsthetic & intellectual capacity.

"to enshrine in" — to put into a shrine.
"to devise = to plan, arrange, and to invent.

The place where a town stands (or stood) is called the SITE (the situation).

to play music — to use an instrument in making music.

$\left.\begin{array}{l}\text{to Moo} \\ \text{to ~~get~~ Low}\end{array}\right\}$ of cattles*.

$\left.\begin{array}{l}\text{to have} \\ \text{to get} \\ \text{to feel}\end{array}\right\}$ a good appetite.

to have a taste (of ~~person~~ thing)
— to have qualities which affect the nerves of the tongue.

to have a taste (of person)
— to have some esthetic & intellectual capacity.

"to enshrine in（—に祀る）" — 神殿に安置すること
"to devise（考察する）" ＝ 計画を立てる、工夫する、発明する

町がたっている（もしくは立っていた）場所はSITE（もしくは敷地）と呼ばれる。

to play music（演奏する） — 音楽を奏でる際に楽器を用いること

$\left.\begin{array}{l}\text{to Moo} \\ \text{to Low}\end{array}\right\}$ of cattle（牛がモーモーと鳴くこと）

$\left.\begin{array}{l}\text{to have} \\ \text{to get} \\ \text{to feel}\end{array}\right\}$ a good appetite（食欲があること）

（物の）味がする
—舌の神経に働きかける性質があること

（人が）審美眼がある
—美的かつ知的な能力があること

---

* cattle（複数形にsはつかない）

A visit to Kawachi.

A visit — a going to a place, or calling upon a person.

A visitation — a coming, generally in a bad sense.

    ex. "A visitation of cholera," — a visitation of famine. Also in a theological sense, a punishment sent by the God.

1. To start up — to jump up suddenly, as from sleep, in a ~~fruit~~ fright.
2. To start or start out —— to begin a journey.
3. To "follow a path" or to go along a path, or to take a path or to pursue a path. But we can't say "to go through a path" for a path is flat.
4. To point to — to show with the finger.
5. To point out — to show with the finger something small in something large — to distinguish by pointing. [crowd.]
   "He pointed out the man to me in the

A visit to Kawachi. A visit — a going to a place, or calling upon a person. A visitation — a coming, generally in a bad sense. 　　EX. "A visitation of cholera" — a visitation of famine.　Also in a theological sense, a punishment sent by the God.	河内訪問 a visit —　ある場所に行くことや、人を訪ねること a visitation —　到来、一般的に悪い意味で 例.「コレラの到来」—飢饉の訪れ 　　また神学上では、神が下す罰のこと

1. To start up — to jump up suddenly, as from sleep, in a ~~friend~~ fright.
2. To start or start out — to begin a journey.
3. "To follow a path" or to go along a path, or to take a path or to pur-sue a path. But we can't say "to go through a path," for path is flat.
4. To point to — to show with the finger.
5. To point out — to show with the finger something small in something large — to distinguish by pointing.　　　[crowd."
" He pointed out the man to me in the

1．to start up（飛び上がる）—突然飛び上がること、眠りからの如く、ぎょっとして、
2．出発する　—　旅に出ること
3．"to follow a path"、もしくは小道に沿っていく、小道を通る、小道を進む。しかし小道は平たんなので"to go through a path"と言うことはできない。
4．To point to —　指で指し示す
5．To point out —　大きいものの中にある小さいものを、識別できるようにするために指で指し示す「彼は人ごみの中でその男を私に指し示した。」

Never use such a phrase as "there were A and A." Instead of — "where were A farmer & his ^family who welcomed us"— we can say,— "where the farmer & his family welcomed us. The "were A" can always be avoided by changing the form of the sentence.

We have justice, art, science, but <u>all that</u> is not what we are proud of. Or —"but our glory is not in those things."

Enterprise — a bold business or undertaking or bold undertaking of any sort. A military enterprise,— a commercial enterprise."

"Adventure" (abstract) — experiences obtained <u>by chance</u> by wandering about, &c.

Fellow countrymen!
Acolyte from Greek Acoleuthos, a follower

Never use such a phrase as "there were
A and A." Insteͣd of — "where were
A farmer & his family who welcomed us" —
we can say, — "where the farmer & his
family welcomed us. The "were A"
can always be avoided by changing
the form of the sentence.

We have justice, art, science, <u>but all
that is not what we are proud of</u>, or
〃 but our glory is not in those things.
Enterprise — a bold business or
　　　undertaking, or bold under-
　　　taking of any sort.　A military
　　　enterprise, — a commercial enter-
　　　prise."

"Adventure" (abstract) — experiences obtain-
　　　ed <u>by chance</u> by wandering
　　　about, etc.

Fellow countrymen !
　　　小僧
　　Acolyte from Greek Acolouthos "a follower"

"there were A and A"というような表現は決して使わないこと。"where were A farmer"（文法的に間違い）と言う代わりに「そこで農夫とその家族が私を歓迎してくれた」（正しい文法）と言うことができる。この"were A"は、文の形を変えることによって使わずに済む。

我々には正義や、芸術、科学があるが、<u>しかしそのどれも我々が誇りとするものではない</u>。我々の栄誉はそれらの中にはないのだ。
Enterprise　──　大胆な事業や仕事、
　　　　　　　　もしくはあらゆる種類の大
　　　　　　　　胆な企て。軍事的な企み
　　　　　　　　── 商業的な言葉

Adventure（抽象詞）── <u>放浪などして偶然得た経験</u>

我が同胞よ！
小僧
Acolyte（従者）は"a follower"を意味するギリシャ語のAcolouthosからきている。

"The country"(1) — the land inhabited by a whole nation — Japan.
"The country"(2) — As opposed to city. Outside of and at a distance from the city.

God made the country, but man made the town. — proverb.

idiom.
"Walk OVER" — This curious idiom is used only with reference to short distances, the original idea being that of crossing a street, or a bridge. Ex. "I'm going over to Mr. Sakurai.

The word "dwarf" — by itself - signifies only an unnaturally small human being. But it is used in compound words to signify other unnaturally small things. Ex. "Dwarf-trees, dwarf-shrubs, dwarf-pines — &c.
We have also the verb "to dwarf" — to make small
Vegitation is dwarfed in the extreme north by the cold.

The country[(1)] — the land inhabited by a whole nation — Japan.
The country[(2)] — As opposed to city. Outside of and at a distance from the city
   God made <u>the</u> country, but man made the town. — proverb.

idiom.
" walk OVER" — This curious idiom is used only with refrence[*1] to short distance, the original idea being that of crossing a street, or a bridge.
   EX. " I'm going over to Mr. Sakurai."

The word "dwarf" — by itself — signifies <u>only</u> an unnaturally small human being. But it is used in compound words to signify ~~hr~~ other unnaturally small things. EX. "Dwarf-trees, dwarf-shrubs, dwarf-pines — etc.
We have also the verb "to dwarf" — to make small
   Vegitation[*2] is dwarfed in the extreme north by the cold.

国家　—　国民全体が居住する土地―日本
田舎　—　都市の反対。都市の外側にあり、離れたところにある。
　神は田園を作り、人は都市を作った
　　―ことわざ

慣用句
"walk OVER"　—　この興味深い慣用句は短い距離のことを言う場合にのみ用いられ元々は道や橋を渡る、というイメージであった。
例．桜井氏のところへ行ってきます。

"dwarf"という語は、それ自体は、不自然に小さい人間のみを示す。しかし、他の語と併せて使うことで、不自然に小さいものを示すのに使われる。例）"Dwarf-trees（盆栽）""dwarf-shrubs（低木）""dwarf-pines（小さい松）"など。
また、"dwarf"―小さくする―という動詞もある。
　植物は極北の地で寒さによって小さくなっている。

---

*1 reference
*2 vegetation

As it were = like, almost like — so to say.
"There in the wood he saw as it were a great fire (something that looked like a great fire)" — correct use.

persons	nouns	verbs
no corresponding word.	Revolt	to revolt
Rebels	rebellion	to rebel
Insurgents	uprising	to uprise
Revolutionaries	Revolution	to make revolution
Insurgents	insurrection	

Exterpate (ex + stirps — Latin — a root) —
to completely destroy.
to give a banquet to —
to grant — to give, to give by word
to give — to give by word or to agree
to consent — to agree to only.

From this time — (requires that mention of a continuous action after it).

(is) understood

As it were = like, almost like — so to say —
    "There in the wood he saw as it were a great fire (something that looked like a great fire) — correct use

persons.	nouns.	verbs.
no corresponding word	Revolt	to revolt
Rebels	rebellion	to rebel
Insurgents from the insurgence to rise against	uprising	to uprise
Revolutionaries	revolution	to make revolution
Insurgents	insurrection	

Extirpate (ex & stirps — Latin — a root) — to completely destroy.
to give a banquet to —
to grant — ~~to give~~, to give by word.
to give — to give by word, or to agree
to consent — to agree to (only).

From this time — (requires that mention of a continuous action after it).

to consecrate = (to make sacred to) — to devote a person or a thing to the Gods.

to enshrine = to preserve sacredly within a shrine.

This word shrine corresponds somewhat to the Japanese miya; though it also corresponds to the word butsudan — But it corresponds more with miya, because it has 2 meanings — 1st. The little box, or case in which the sacred object is kept.

2nd. The temple itself in which the shrine is kept.

to worship = to address with prayer, like God — To ask help divine from.

to reverence = to show religious respect to — to bow before piously, to honour religiously.

to consecrate = (to make sacred to) —
         to devote a person or a thing to the
         Gods.

to enshrine = to preserve sacredly within
   a shrine.
       This word <u>shrine</u> corresponds
   somewhat to the Japanese <u>miya</u>;
    though it also corresponds to the word
    <u>butsudan</u>. But it corresponds
   more with <u>miya</u> because it has
   2 meanings — 1 <u>st</u>. The little
   box, or case in which the sacred
   objects is* kept.
   2nd. The temple itself in which
   the shrine is kept.

to worship = to address with prayer — like
                help
        God. To ask ⸨divine from.

to reverence = to show religious respect to
   — to bow before piously, to honour
     religiously.

to consecrate ＝（−に対して聖なるものに
    する、という意）
    人や物を神々に捧げる

to enshrine ＝神殿の内部に神聖に安置する
    この shrine という語は日本語の「宮」
    にほぼ同じである。
    だが仏壇という語にもまた対応する。
    しかし次の二つの意味を持つので、宮
    の方がより合致している。一つ目は、
    神聖なものを入れる小さい箱や入れ物
    二つ目は、聖なるものを入れた箱が安
    置される寺院それ自体

to worship ＝祈りの言葉を述べること、例
    えば神に神助を乞うこと。

to reverence ＝ 信心を示すこと
    ―その前で信心深くおじぎをし、宗教
    的に尊敬すること

---

* are

A Japanese answers "Yes", or "No" to the negative or the affirmative contained in a question.

An Englishman does not. He answers the fact,—not to the words of the question.

I think you have no vacation in April, have you?
Yes — (we have).

I think you have a vacation in April, have you not?
Yes.

You have not written any composition for me, have you?
No — (not written).

The main point to remember is that only the FACT should be stated by the answer.

You did not hear any news of Mr. Kano today, did you?
No.

In such answers remember that
Yes means IS
No " IS NOT.

A Japanese answers "Yes", or "No" to
the negative or the affirmative <u>contained in
a question</u>.
　An Englishman does not. He answers the
fact, — not to the words of the question.

I think you have no vacation in April,
　have you ?
　Yes — (we have).
I think you have a vacation in April,
　have you not?
　Yes.
You have not written any composition for me,
　have you ?
　No　— (not written)
The main point to remember is that
　only the FACT should be stated by
　the answer.
You did not hear any news of Mr. Kano
　today, did you ?
　<u>No</u>.
In such answers remember that
　Yes　means　IS
　No　　〃　　IS NOT.

　　　　　　　　　　日本人は質問に含まれる否定や肯定に対して
「はい」や「いいえ」と返答するが、それは
<u>質問文そのものに対する</u>答である。
　イギリス人はそうしない。質問文の言葉に
対してではなく、事実に対し返答する。

四月に休日はありませんよね？
　ありますか？
　Yes（いいえ）―（あります）
四月に休日はありますよね？
　ありませんか？
　Yes（はい、あります）
僕の為の作文をまだ何も書いていないんだね？
　No（はい）―（書いていない）

覚えておくべき重要な点は、事実のみを答え
によって示すべきだ、ということである

今日嘉納さんの消息は聞いてないですね？
　<u>No（はい）</u>

このような返答の場合、
　Yes　とは　後に続くのは肯定文
　No　とは　後に続くのが否定文
　であることを覚えておかなくてはならない

1. All matters sent through a post office is called by the general name of Mail. The Government does not carry the mail for nothing, does it?
   No — (does NOT carry)
2. There is no fire in the stove today, is there? No.
3. I think there is fire in the stove, is there not? No.
   (The fact is to be stated by the answer, — not the correctness or incorrectness of the question.)
4. I think time is not the kite flying season, is it? Yes; (it is).
5. "None of you will graduate this year, will you?"
   "Oh yes — we will."
   "I don't think we will have (we won't have) any snow this year, will we?"
   "No, — no more."
   I think you are not all studying Latin, are you?
   "No, — we are not."

1 All matters sent through a post office
  is* called by the general name of Mail.
  The Ger^over nment does not carry the mail
  for nothing, does it?
                No — (does NOT carry)

2 There is no fire in ^the stove today, is
  there?   No.

3 I think there is fire in the stove, is
  there not?   No.
     (The fact is to be stated by the answer,
  — not the correctness or incorrectness of
  the question.)

4. I think time is not the kite flying
   season, is it ?   Yes; (it is).

5. "None of you will graduate this year,
   will you ?"
     "Oh Yes — we will."
   "I don't think we will have (we won't
   have) any snow this year, will we ?"
     "No, — no more.
   — I think you ~~are~~ are not all
   studying Latin, are you?
        "No," — we are not.

---

* are

1 郵便局を通して配達される物は全て、
  Mail 郵便物という一般的な名称で呼ばれる。
政府は無料で郵便物を運んではくれないですよね？
  No（はい）—（配達しません）
2 今日はストーブに火はついていないですよね？
  No（はい、ついていません）
3 ストーブに火がついていますよね？ついていませんか？
  No（はい、ついていません）
  （返答によって示すべきは事実であり
  — その質問が正しいか正しくないかではない）
4 凧揚げの季節ではないですよね？
  Yes（いいえ、凧揚げの季節です）
5 「今年はあなた方は誰も卒業しないですよね？」
  「Oh Yes（いえいえ）—卒業しますよ」
  「今年は雪はもう降らないですよね？」
  「No（はい）—もう降らないです」
— あなた方みんながラテン語を勉強しているのではないですよね？
  「No（はい）」—勉強していません

Paper-money is <u>never</u> used in the plural. It is an abstract, or general term.

A particular piece of paper-money is called A BILL.

A bill for one yen, dollar or a one-dollar bill

Thus compounds are formed — a 5-dollar bill
        a 10-dollar "
        a hundred dollar bill.

English money in paper is called Notes.
  A one-pound note, a 10-pound note.
A bill for 100 francs. This might mean a Kanjō-kaki. It is better to say "a 100-franc bill."

Paper-money is <u>never</u> used in the plural. It is an abstract, or general term.

 A particular piece of paper-money is called A BILL.

 A bill for one yen, dollar or a
  one-dollar bill

Thus compounds
 are formed — a 5-dollar bill
    a 10-dollar 〃
     a hundred-dollar bill.

English money in paper is called Notes.
  A one-pound note, a 10-pound note.

A bill for 100 francs. This might mean
 a kanjo-kaki.* It is better to say
  a 100-franc bill."

Paper money 紙幣は複数形で使われることは決してない。この語は抽象名詞、もしくは総称である。

 ある特定の紙幣は A BILL と呼ばれる。

 1円札、1ドル紙幣、もしくは1ドルの紙幣

したがって、複合語が作られる
   —5ドル札
    10ドル札
    100ドル札

英国の紙幣は Notes と呼ばれる。
  1ポンド札、10ポンド札

100 フランの Bill（請求書）
この語は勘定書きを意味することもある。
a 100- franc bill（100 フラン札）と言う方が良い。

＊勘定書（かんじょうがき）のこと

tired out by the work of preparing English studies.

The effects of outer influence upon the body, are often expressed in English by a peculiar reflex idiom, with the use of the personal pronoun as object.

Ex.

"I heard a sound which made ME feel as if MY ears were being pierced by a gimlet."

"The heat MADE ME feel as if I was going to melt all away."

This form is especially used when a part of the body is referred to, instead of the whole.

"The blow made me feel as if my arm had been cut off."

"The cold made me feel as if I had no feet."

tired out by the work of preparing English studies.

英語の勉強の準備で疲れ果てた

The effects of outer influence upon the body, are ~~usually~~ ^often expressed in English by a peculiar reflex idiom, with the use of the personal pronoun as object.
　EX.
　"I heard a sound which mad* ME feel as if MY ears were being pierced by a gimlet."
　　"The heat MADE ME feel as if I was going to melt all away."
　This form is especially used when a part of the body is referred to, instead of the whole.
　　"The blow made me feel as if my arm had been cut off."
　　"The cold made me feel as if I had no feet."

外部からの刺激が体に及ぼす影響は英語ではしばしば、人称代名詞を目的語とする特有の再帰の語法で表現される。

例）
「私の耳が錐で貫かれるような感じの音を聞いた。」
「暑さで体がすっかり溶けてしまいそうな感じだった。」

この用法は、体全体ではなく、体の一部について述べる時に特に使われる。
「その一打で、まるで私の腕が切り落とされたかのように感じた。」
「寒くてまるで足が無くなってしまったかのように感じた。」

---

* made

Don't use such expression as —
— "made me feel pleasantly."
— "I felt very pleasant."
— except in particular meanings.
They are only used (in _conversation_), to
express bodily satisfaction — otherwise
difficult to describe.

    The effects of anything causing
pleasure must be described by other
idioms whenever possible.

    But the noun "pleasure" may always
be used with appropriate verbs &
adjectives.
— "The sound gave me a THRILL of pleasure."
— "The news thrilled us without joy."
— "The mere sound of his voice gave
    me a thrill of joy."

Another very useful verb to use instead
of those phrases I find fault with, is
TO CHARM —
    Lat. "carmen" (a song, but anciently
        a _magical song_.)
ex. —
    "I was charmed by the story."

Don't use such expression as —
— "made me feel pleasantly.
— " I felt very pleasant."
— except in particular meanings.
They are only used (in conversation), to
express bodily satisfaction — otherwise
difficult to describe.

The effects of anything causing
pleasure must be described by other
idioms whenever possible.
But the noun "pleasure" may always
be used with appropriate verbs &
adjectives.
— "The sound gave me a THRILL of pleasure."
— "The news thrilled us without joy."
— "The mere sound of his voice gave
me a thrill of joy."

Another very useful verb to use instead
of those phrases I find fault with, is
TO CHARM.
Lat.* "Carmen" (a song, but anciently
a magical song.)
EX.—
"I was charmed by the story."

以下のような表現はしないように
— "made me feel pleasantly"
— " I felt very pleasant"
— 特別な意味を除いて
（会話などで）身体的に満足していることを表す時にのみ使われる。—それ以外には表現しにくい。

喜びがもたらされた状態を述べるときはなるべく、他の慣用句で表さなくてはいけないしかし"pleasure"という名詞は常に適切な動詞や形容詞と共にならいつでも使うことができる。
「その音は私にぞくぞくするような喜びを与えた」
「その知らせに私たちを喜ぶどころか、ただ震えあがった。」
「彼の声だけで私はわくわくするような喜びを感じた」
私が問題があるとしてとがめた表現の代わりに使える非常に便利な動詞が
TO CHARM である
ラテン語の「カルメン」（歌のこと、しかし古くは魔法の歌のことであった）
例）
「私はその話に魅了された」

---
* Latin の略

"The beauty of the landscape charm_ed_"
"He is a charm_ing_ gentleman."
"Norman had a _more_ charm_ing_ manner."
"Some Japanese poems are very charm_ing_."
"I was charm_ed_ by that music."

"Enchant" is still stronger.
We cannot say "an enchant_ing_ man"
though we can say "a charming man"
— because it would be extravagant.
But we can say "an enchant_ing_ landscape."

A third good word for you to use, is the verb TO DELIGHT — used both passively & actively, and its adjectives &c.
Instead of "I feel pleasant," (which is bad) — say "I AM DELIGHTED."
or "This is delightful, I feel delight_ed_."

"This delighted me" (no preposition):
"The music delighted him."

The verb amuse must never used

"The beauty of the landscape charmed."
"He is a charming gentleman."
"No man had a more charming manner."
"Some Japanese poems are very charming."
"I was charmed by that music."
"Enchant" is still stronger.
We cannot say "an enchanting man,"
though we can say " a charming man",
— because it would be extravagant.
But we can say " an enchanting land-
scape."

  A third good word for you to use,
is the verb TO DELIGHT. — used both
passively & actively, and its adjective etc.
  Instead of " I feel pleasant," (which
is bad) — say "I AM DELIGHTED."
or "This is delightful, I feel delighted."
" This delighted me." (no preposition):
The music delighted him."

The verb amuse must never * used
   文ノ差 アリ
    chess

「その風景の美しさに魅了された」
「彼は魅力的な紳士だ」
「あんなに魅力的な物腰の人はいなかった」
「日本の詩にはとても魅力的なものがある」
「私はその音楽に魅了された」
"Enchant（魅惑する）"はずっと強い語である。
"an enchanting man"と言うことはできないが"a charming man（魅力的な男性）"と言うことはできる―なぜなら、誇張になってしまうであろうから。
しかし"an enchanting landscape（うっとりするような風景）"と言うことはできる。

3つめの使うべき良い単語は、TO DELIGHTである。―受動態でも能動態でも両方、その形容詞なども使われる。
"I feel pleasant"（これは悪い例）と言う代わりに"I am delighted（私は喜んでいる）"もしくは"This is delightful（これは喜ばしい）" "I feel delighted（私は嬉しく思う）"と言う。
"This delighted me（このことは私を楽しませた）"（前置詞なし）
: 彼はその音楽を楽しんだ。

真剣な場面では動詞 amuse は決して使ってはならない。 チェス*

---

* be が入る

*チェスならば動詞の amuse を使ってもよいという例として、ここにチェスと記したのではあるまいか。

seriously. Children amuse themselves with toys, but men can not amuse themselves with mathematics, or philosophy, or art, or science, or statesmanship. Nor can they amuse themselves with high forms of beauty.

To enjoy —
To enjoy myself —
To take enjoyment } in —
To   "   pleasure }
To divert oneself —
To pass the time in —
To entertain oneself —
To be entertained by —
To take satisfaction — (in)
To take relaxation in —

These terms can be used instead of "To amuse."

There are few words about which the students make more frequent mistakes, than the word CHARACTER.

Character does not mean (in a person) any one particular idiosyncrasy, peculiarity, tendency or sentiment. It means the

seriously. Children amuse themselves with toys, but men can not <u>amuse</u> themselves with mathematics, or philosophy, or art, or science, or statemanship*

Nor can they <u>amuse</u> themselves with high forms of beauty.

        Those terms can be used instead of "To amuse."

To enjoy —
To enjoy myself —
To take enjoyment } in —
To 〃   pleasure
To divert oneself —
To pass the time in —
To entertain oneself —
To be entertained by —
To take satisfaction — (in)
To take relaxation in —

There are few words about which the students make more frequent mistakes, than the word CHARACTER.

   Character does not mean (in a person) any one particular idiosyncrasy, peculiarity, tendency, or sentiment. It means the

---

* statesmanship

子供はおもちゃ遊びをして楽しむ (amuse)、しかし大人は数学や哲学、芸術、科学、政治的手腕を<u>楽しむ</u> (amuse) ことはできない。また高尚な美を楽しむ (amuse) こともできない。

      以下の語は
      "to amuse" の代
      わりに
      使うことができる

to enjoy
to enjoy myself –
to take enjoyment } in — （—を楽しむ）
to 〃   pleasure
to divert oneself –
to pass the time in –
to entertain oneself –
to be entertained by – （—に楽しまされる）
to take satisfaction –(in)　（—に満足する）
to take relaxation in – （—で息抜きをする）

CHARACTER（性格）という語ほど学生が頻繁に間違える語はあまりない。

   Character という語は、人が持つある特定の特徴や特質、傾向、心情などを意味するものではない。

quality of the whole sum of feelings, impulses, tendencies, both good or bad. It is the result of the addition of all these. We can speak of a particular tendency being in a man's character; but we cannot say it is the character.

The nearest synonym to 'character' is 'disposition',— although this word is more limited in meaning — viz. the general inclination of character.

Neither is 'character' an exact equivalent of 'nature', although nature is often used for it by common people. Nature refers less to mental than to moral & physical inclination.

"Patriotism" says one of my class, "is a natural character." Here the word is wrong,— because patriotism is one sentiment, and one sentiment is not character. What he should say is "Patriotism is a natural (inborn) sentiment, or feeling."

"Characteristic" has a more limited meaning than its noun. It only means "distinguishing."

quality of the whol* sum of feelings, impulses, tendencies, both good or bad. It is the result of the addition of all these.   We can speak of a particular tendency being in a man's character; but we cannot say it is the character.

  The nearest synonym to 'character' is 'disposition', — although this word is more limited in meaning — viz. the general inclination of character.

    Neither is 'character' an exact equivalent of "nature", although nature is often used for it by common people.   Nature refers less to mental than to moral & physical inclination.

  "Patriotism" says one of my class, "is a natural character." Here the word is wrong, — because patriotism is one sentiment, and one sentiment is not character. What he should say is "Patriotism is a natural (inborn) sentiment, or feeling." "Characteristic" has a more limited meaning than its noun. It only means "distinguishing."

---

* whole

"Character" is a abstract noun, capable of being particularized by relation either to persons or things. "The character of Mr. ___ is amiable;" "The chaster of the landscape is dreary."

"It is used in many sciences — geology, botany, &c. "The character of tropical vegitation is luxuriant."

English idiom. The "love of home." The "love of country." In the families (life understood) The understood word explains the use of the article.

Can't say "to make wrong," say, "to do wrong."
"to give way to" — to yield to.
"to give rise to" — to cause.

FLY — FLED — FLED to run away from / to abandon.
FLY — FLEW — FLOWN to move with wings.
"To die away" does not mean "to die at all."
— to diminish gradually — like a sound

'Character' is a*¹ abstract noun, capable of being particularized by relation either to persons or things. "The character of Mr. — is amiable;" "The chacter*² of the landscape is dreary."

" It is used in ~~meaning~~ many sciences — geology, botany, etc. "The character of tropical vegetation*³ is luxuriant."

English idiom. the "love of home."
                the "love of country."

In the family (life). understood The understood word explains the use of the article.

Can't say "to make wrong", say "to do wrong."
"to give way to" — to yield to.
"to give rise to" — to cause.

FLY – FLED – FLED   to run away from—,
                     to abandon.
FLY – FLEW – FLOWN   to move with wings.
" to die away" does not mean "to die at all.
   — to diminish gradually like a sound

---

*1 an
*2 character
*3 vegetation

'Character'「性格」とは抽象名詞で、人や物に関連して、個別的に述べることも可能だ。
「—さんは愛想が良い性格だ」「その土地の特徴はうらさびしいものだ」
「この語は地質学、植物学など多くの自然科学の分野で使われている」「南国の植物の特徴は繁茂しているということだ」

英語の慣用句：「家庭愛」
              「愛国心」

家族（生活）の中で、家庭で。　In the family と定冠詞 the を使うのは In the family life という内容が分かっている言葉だから

"to make wrong" とは言わないので、
"to do wrong" と言わなくてはいけない。
"to give way to" — 譲る
"to give rise to" — 引き起こす

Fly – Fled – Fled　—から逃げる、棄てる
Fly – Flew – Flown　羽根で飛ぶ
"to die away" というのは「死ぬ」という意味ではまったくない
　— 音が消えるように、次第に消えていく、ということ

135

The word "tall" qualifies human beings and trees (and masts of ships) — not other objects as a rule except in poetry. "High" or "lofty" are used instead.

"Lofty" is much greater word than "high". It comes from an ancient English word "lift" meaning the SKY.

A man not tall, but the reverse is called "short". A "low man" means a man of vulgar manners & bad morals, — not a man of low stature. But we can say of "low stature" or "undersized" as well as "short", — or "under middle height."

Men neither tall nor short are said to be "middle height" or "of ordinary height" or "ordinary size" &c.

Notice, in all this, that the word "body" is never used in English, — except in speaking of a dead ~~body man~~.

The variations of weight, breadth, & general ~~size~~ form, are expressed in an infinite variety of words. But two

The word "tall" qulifies*1 human beings and trees (and masts of ships) — not other objects, as a rule except in poetry. "High" or "lofty" are used instead.

　　Lofty is much greater word than "high". It comes from an ancient English word "lift" meaning the SKY.

　A man not tall, but the reverse is called "short". A "low man" means a man of vulgar manners and mad morals, — not a man of low stature. But we can say of "low stature" or "undersized" as well as "short", — or "under middle height."

Man neither tall nor short are said to be "of middle height" or "of ordinary height" or "ordinary size" etc.
Notice, in all this, that the word "body" is never used in English, — except in speaking of 　a dead ~~body~~ man.

The variations of weight, breadth, & general ~~size~~ form, are expressed in an infinate*2 variety of words. But two

---

*1 qualifies
*2 infinite

137

words are especially used, — the verb "to build" and the curious noun "build" (meaning frame, architecture." They are used thus: Illustrative idioms.
"He is a man of powerful build."
" He is powerfully built."
"He is a feebly built man."
He is a man of weak build.
He is of slim (or slender) build.
He is strongly, gracefully, heavily — &c.
He is well built.
He is badly, clumsily, awkwardly, &c.

The word KNIT is also used of men.
  He is strongly knit } i.e. fastened or
  He is well   "   } knotted together.
  "   " badly   "

The term "fat" has in modern English conversation a rather contemptible meaning. So its use is avoided. Instead of saying "He is very fat," we say "he is rather stout," which is a flattering way of saying the same thing.

— "A large man" does not mean a fat man, — but a man of great breadth,

words are especially used, — the verb 'to build' and the curious noun "build" (meaning <u>frame</u>, architecture". They are used thus: Illustrative idioms.
"He is a man of powerful build."
or "He is powerfully built."
 "He is a feebly built man."
 He is a man of weak <u>builded</u>.
He is of slim (or slender) build.
 built
He is strongly, gracefully, heavily — etc.
He is well built.
He 〃 badly, clumsily, awkwardly, etc.
The word KNIT is also used of men.
 He is strong knit.) i.e. fastened or
 He 〃 well 〃 } <u>Knotted</u> together.
 〃 〃 badly 〃)

The term 'fat' has in modern English conversation a rather contemptible meaning. So its use is avoided. Instead of saying "He is very fat," we say "he is rather stout;" which is a flattering way of saying the same thing.
 — "A large man" does not mean a fat man, — but a man of great <u>breadth</u>,

しかし、次の二つの語が特に使われる。— "to build" という動詞と、(枠組みや構造を意味する) "build" という不思議な名詞だ。それらは次のように使われる。 実例となる慣用句。
「彼は逞しい体格の男だ」
もしくは「彼は体つきが逞しく出来ている」
「彼は貧相な作りの男だ」
彼は弱そうな体つきの男だ。
彼は細身だ。

彼は力強い、優美な、どっしりと（した体格）
—など
彼は体格が良い。

彼は体格が悪い、不恰好だ、ぶざまだ、など。
KNITという語もまた男性に使われる。
彼はがっちり引き締まった体だ。｜つまり、固く締まっている
彼はよく引き締まった体だ。 ｜結びあわされている
彼はだらしがない体だ。

'fat' という語は、現代の英会話では、やや軽蔑的な意味を持っている、
それゆえあまり使われない。"He is very fat" という代わりに、"he is rather stout（彼はかなり恰幅が良い）" と、同様のことを言うにも褒めて言う。
— "a large man" は太った男のことは指さない。—横幅が大きく、

139

and strength of body. He may be very thin and yet large.

A man both small of stature and small of frame, is simply called "a little man" or "a small man" "undersized", "Under middle (size/height)" is often used.

FRAME can be used instead of BUILD.

It is not customary ever to speak of "The build of a woman," but only of a man. A woman is said to be "well-formed" or "to have a pretty figure" (i.e. body) This word figure might never used in speaking of a man.

Among words in common use to denote peculiarities of build the following should be learned:—

1. "Tough" — A tough man — a man of hard flesh & great strength.

[This word, although used even by the poorest peasantly, is also used in by poets.

"Cyril ....,
Tough, supple, sinew-corded, apt,
But tougher, stronger, heavier, he that smote,"

and <u>strength</u> of body. He may be very thin and yet large.

A man both small of stature and small of frame, is simply called " a little man" or "a small man" "undersized"; "Under middle $\begin{pmatrix} \text{size} \\ \text{height} \end{pmatrix}$ is often used.

<u>FRAME</u> can be used instead of BUILD.

It is not customary ever to speak of "The build" of a woman, but only of a man. A woman is said to be "well-formed" or "to have a pretty <u>figure</u>" (i.e. body) This word figure might never *¹ used in speaking of a man.

Among words in common use to denot*² peculialities*³ of build, the following should be learned:—

1. "Tough" — A tough man — a man of hard flesh & great strength.

　　[This word, although used even by the poorest peasantly*⁴, is also used ~~vi~~ by poets.

　　　　　Cyril............,

<u>Tough</u>, supple, sinew corded, apt,
But <u>tougher</u>, stronger, heavier, he that smote,

がっちりした体格の男性を指す。
とても痩せていても横幅が大きいことはある。
身長が低く、かつ小柄な男は単に "a little man" や "a small man"、もしくは "undersized" と呼ばれる。
中肉中背よりも小さい、という表現がよく使われる。

FRAME という語は BUILD の代わりに使うことができる。
女に対して "the build" と言うことはこれまで慣習的になく、男に対してのみ使われる。
女は "well-formed（スタイルが良い）" や "to have a pretty figure（スタイルが良い）" と言われる（figure とはつまり body のこと）。
この figure という語は男のことを話す際には用いられないかもしれない。
体格の特徴を記すのによく用いる言葉のうち、以下の語を学ばなくてはいけない。

１．"Tough" ― たくましい男 ― 強靭な肉体と強さを持った男

　　［この語は最下層の農民も使うし、詩人もまた使う］
シリル・・・
たくましく、しなやかさ、筋骨隆々、武技に優れていた
しかし、彼を殴り、投げ飛ばした男は、

---

*1 be を入れる
*2 denote
*3 peculiarities
*4 peasantry

And threw him." — Tennyson; "The Princess."
2. Gaunt — a very powerful word, meaning, and strong, without flesh (sometimes, like the word "Thin," it may mean "wasted."
3. Lanky — Long and thin and clumsy.
4. Jawky — Extremely clumsy, in shape & action.

The word "complexion" is used commonly instead of "skin" in describing persons. But it has a wider meaning than skin. The word "white" is not used commonly to describe a white skin. "A White man" does not refer to a man whose skin is white, but who belongs to white is called the "white RACE.

Instead of white we use the ancient word "fair." "Fair" has 2 meanings, — "white," & "beautiful." Thus we say "a fair day" (in poetry.) "A fair woman" — a beautiful woman, irrespective of colour.

But usually, in speaking of persons today "fair" is used to describe whiteness of skin & light colour of hair. This use of the word, too, is very old. The Norwegian king's name "Harold Haarfager" signifies "Harold Fair Hair." His hair was of

And threw him. "— Tennyson, - The Princess,"
2. Gaunt — a very powerful word, meaning, and strong, without flesh (sometimes, like the word – Thin," it may mean "wasted"
3. Lanky — Long and thin and clumsy
4. Gawky — Extremely clumsy, in shape & action,

The word "complexion" is used commonly instead of 'skin' in describing persons. But it has a wider meaning than skin.
The word 'white' is not used commonly to describe a white skin . "a White man" does not refer to a man whose skin is white, but who belongs to white is called the white RACE.

Instead of white we use the ancient word "fair". 'Fair' has 2 meanings, — (1) white, (2) beautiful. Thus we say "a fair day" (in poetry.)
"A fair woman" — a beautiful woman, irrespectible*1 of colour.
But usually, in speaking at persons today " fair " is used to describe whiteness of skin & light colour of hair. This use of the word, too, is very old. The Norwegian king's name "Harold Haarfago" signifies "Harold Fair Hair", "His fair*2 was of

---

*1 irrespective
*2 hair

a very bright colour.

In comparison we say, "Of the two John is the fairest but Phillips the handsomest" (or vice versa.)

"Dark" the opposite of "fair" is similarly used. It is a totally different word from "black" with which it must never be confused. It refers to a brown tint of skin. Sometimes this brown is a rich fruit colour, so that we use the adjective "olive" to describe Italian & Spanish skins. Sometimes it is much deeper and is called "swarthy." Dark hair, in English, does not necessarily mean black hair: it means brown hair or chestnut-colored hair — as opposed to golden or to red or to straw-colored hair.

To describe women (not men) the English has borrowed two words from the French, "blonde", and "brunette" representing types of fair & of dark women. These words are never used of men — except by the vulgar.

Dark color given to the skin by exposure to the sun is called "tan" or "sunburn."

"He is tanned." "He is sunburnt." The word "weather-beaten" does not refer to color, but to surface. It means "worn by weather."

a very bright colour.

   In comparison we say "Of the two, John is the fairest but Phillip the handsomest" (or vice versa)

   "Dark" the opposite of "fair" is similarly used. It is a totally different word from "black" with which it must never be confused. It refers to a brown tint of skin. Sometimes this brown is a rich fruit-color, — so that we use the adjective "olive" to describe Italian & Spanish skins. Sometimes it is much deeper and is called "swarthy". Dark hair, in English, does not necessarily mean black hair: it means brown hair or chestnut-colored hair — as opposed to golden or to red or to straw colored hair.

   To describe women (<u>not</u> men) the English have borrowed two words from the French, "blonde", and "brunette" representing types of fair & of dark woman. These words are never used of men — except by the vulgar.

   Dark color given to the skin by exposure to the sun is called "tan" or "sunburn".
      "He is tanned." "He is sunburnt"
The word "weather beaten" does not refer to <u>color</u>, — but to surface. It means "worn by weather."

Family — from ancient oscan language
— famul, a house. — since.
Latin "familia" a family.
Familiar "(does not mean)
of the family but only very intimate."
"I have a family" in English conversation does
not mean that "I have a father & mother,
brothers and sisters." It means only "I have
a wife and children." "I have no family"
means, "I have no wife and children."

The fact alone shows the vast difference
in Western society. It is not the custom for
children to support their parents; neither is
it the custom for parents to support their children after a certain age. The family breaks
up as the children grow up, and scatter in
all directions.

As a consequence, the most important
things for a man or woman in life, is to be
able to marry. For unless he or she can
marry, he or she can have no home. Not to have a
home is a hardship. Therefore English novels
are mostly written about love and marriage,
and things which to intelligent orientals
seem foolish and nonsensical.

Family — from ancient Oscan language
— <u>famus</u>, a house. — lives.
Latin "familia" a family,
(does not mean)
familiar of the family but only <u>very</u> intimate;
"I have a family." in English conversation does not mean that I have a father & mother, brothers and sisters. It means only "I have a wife and children." "I have no family." means, "I have no wife and children."

The fact alone shows the vast difference in Western society. It is not the custom for children to support his parents, neither is it the custom for parents to support their children after a certain age. The family breaks up as the children grow up, and scatter in all directions.

As a consequence, the most important things for a man or woman in life, is to be able to marry. For unless he or she can ~~marry,~~ *he or she can have no home. Not to have a home is a hardship. Therefore English novels are mostly written about love and marriage, and things which to intelligent Orientals seem foolish and nonsensical.

---

* 下の marry を消去しない、の意か

Family ─ 家や人生を意味する古代オスク語 famus
家族を意味するラテン語 familia から来ている。

familiar は家族の、という意味ではなく、ただ、とても親しい、馴染みがある、という意味。

英会話において、"I have a family（私には家族がいる）"というのは私には父や母、兄弟や姉妹がいるということを意味するわけではない。単に「私には妻と子がいる」ということを意味する。"I have no family（私には家族がいない）"は「私には妻も子もいない」ことを意味する。

この事実だけで、西洋社会がいかに大きく異なっているかが分かる。子供が親を扶養するという慣習はなく、又親が子がある一定の年齢に達した後も生活を扶養するという慣習もない。家族は子供が成長するとバラバラになり、別々の方向へと散っていく。

結果的に、男にとっても女にとっても、人生において最も重要なことは、結婚できることである。結婚できなければ、家庭を持つことができないからだ。家庭を持たないというのは辛いことである。したがって英国小説は大半が愛と結婚、そして、知的な東洋人にとってはばかげていて無意味であるように思えるような事柄ばかりについて書かれている。

The fact that parents and children, brothers and relatives, do not help each other, makes life much more difficult. There is only exception. As daughters are not able to earn their own living, they are taken care of until old enough to marry.

Here again comes a great difference in customs. Parents (in English-speaking countries) do not arrange marriages. The young men and women marry just as they please. Once married, they have nothing more to do with the lives of their parents.

Children have no duty to their parents after coming of age — by law. This term is 18 years for girls, and 21 years for men.

Once married, the idea of living with parents is rarely entertained. A man will not live with his mother-in-law if he can help it, nor a woman with the parents of her husband. The very word "mother-in-law" is a term for laughter in the West. Comic songs are written about it. Here is an

The fact that parents and children, brothers and relatives, do not help each other, makes life much more difficult. There is only exception. As daughters are not able to earn their own living, they are taken care of until old enough to marry.

　Here again comes a great difference in customs. Parents (in English-speaking countries) do not arrange marriages. The young men and women marry just as they pleases. Once married, they have nothing more to do with the life of their parents.

　Children have no duty to their parents after coming of age — by law. This term is 18 years for girls, and 21 years for men.

　Once married, the idea of living with parents is rarely entertained. A men* will not live with his mother-in-law if he can help it, nor a woman with the parents of her husband. The very word "mother-in-law" is a term for laughter in the West. Comic songs are written about it. Here is an

両親や子供、兄弟や親族がお互い助け合わないという現実は人生をずっと困難なものにしている。一つだけ例外がある。娘は自分の食い扶持を稼ぐことができないため、彼女たちは結婚できる年齢になるまで面倒を見てもらう。

　ここにまた大きな慣習の違いがある。両親（英語を話す国では）は結婚相手を世話しない。若い男女は自分たちが好きなように結婚する。
いったん結婚すると、彼らは自分の両親の暮らしとは一切関係がなくなる。

　子供は成年後は両親に対しては何の義務もない　―法的には。
この成年とは、女子では十八歳、男子では二十一歳である。

　いったん結婚すると、両親と同居するという考えはめったに受け入れられない。男性は義理の母親とできるならば暮したくはないし、女性も夫の両親と暮らそうとはしない。この "mother-in-law" という言葉そのものが西洋では笑いの対象である。歌にも面白おかしく歌われている。

---

* man

example, — of a common kind: —

— "He stood on his head on the wild seashore,
And joy was the cause of the act;
He felt as he never had felt before —
Insanely glad, in fact.
And why? Because on that very day,
His mother-in-law had sailed
To a tropical country far away
Where tigers and snakes prevailed."

So the family thus breaks up — disintegrates, and as the rule is "every one for himself," — there is very little respect for old age, — very little reverence for parents. On the other hand, there is great reverence for young women & girls. A man in America thinks he must not even sit down if a girl is standing up. This is, of course, the result of the obsolete freedom give to women.

In England, the law of primogeniture parents, among the wealthy classes, those extreme of family disintegration to be found in America & the Colonies.

example, — of a common kind: —
　— "He stood on his head on the wild seashore,
　And joy was the cause of the act;
　He felt as he never had felt before —
　Insanely glad, in fact.
　And why? Because on that very day,
　His mother-in-law had sailed.
　To a tropical country far way
　where tigers and snakes prevailed."
　　As the family thus breaks up — dis-
integrates, and as the rule is "every one
for himself," — there is very little respect
for old age, — very little reverence for
parents. On the other hand, there is great
reverence for young woman*1 & girls.
A man in America thinks he must not
even sit down if a girl is standing up.
This is, of course, the result of the obsolete
　freedom give*2 to women.

　　In England, the law of primogeniture
parents, among the wealthy classes, those streams
of family disintegration to be formed in
America & the Colonies.

ここに一般的な例を挙げる。
—男は波が荒れ狂う海辺で逆立ちをした
喜びのあまり、そんな行動をとったのだ
これまでそう感じたことのないほどに—
実際、狂ったように嬉しかった。
なぜか？　まさにその日に
義理の母親が船旅に出たからだ。
虎と蛇がたくさんいる
はるか遠くの熱帯の国へと出たからだ。
　こうして家族は別れてばらばらになる
そして「みなそれぞれ自分自身の為に」とい
う原則で。—老人に対する敬意はほとんどな
い—両親にたいする敬愛の念もほとんどない。
その一方で、若い女性や少女に対しての敬愛
の念は非常にある。
アメリカの男性は、もし若い娘が立っている
ならば自分は座っていたりしてはいけないと
考える。
これは当然ながら、女性に与えられた時代遅
れな「自由」の考え方の結果である。
　イギリスでは、長子相続の法律が裕福な階
級において家族の余計者を生み出し家庭から
はじきだされた人々がアメリカや植民地に行
くことになる。

---

*1 women
*2 given

5th May

Literature, in the general sense, means the whole mass of works written in one language upon all subjects. Thus "Japanese Literature" in this sense includes all books written in the language.

But "Literature" in the special and more correct sense refers only to those works in which the language is artificially constructed so as to express the thought of the writer in the best possible way. And even this definition is too wide. For history, philosophy, science, and law do not properly belong to pure literature, but form lesser special literatures by themselves. Literature, pure and simple, includes only works representing the artistic use of language for the purposes of teaching emotional truth and beauty.

The object of pure literature is to affect the emotions. It does this especially through poetry and through fiction.

"Style" is the particular manner in which the emotion is expressed. It is

8th/ May   Literature, in the <u>general</u> sense, means the whole mass of works written in one language upon all subjects. Thus "Japanese Literature" in this sense includes all books written in the language.

But "Literature" in the special and more correct sense refers only to those works in which the language is artificially constructed so as to express the thought of the writer in the best possible way. And even this definition* is too wide. For history, philosophy, science, and law do not properly belong to pure literature, but form lesser special literatures by themselves. Literature, pure and simple, includes only works representing the artistic use of language for the purposes of teaching emotional truth and beauty.

The object of pure literature is to affect the emotions. It does this especially through poetry and through fiction.

"Style" is the particular manner in which the emotion is expressed. It is

---

* definition

5月8日　一般的には、文学とはある言語ですべての題材について書かれた作品すべてのことを意味する。従って、この意味において「日本文学」とはその言語（日本語）で書かれた全ての本を含む。

しかし、特別かつより正確な意味では、「文学」とは、作者が自分の考えを可能な限りもっとも良い方法で表現するために言葉を巧みに構成している作品のみを指す。

しかし、この定義ですら広すぎる。歴史、哲学、科学、法律は正確には純文学には属さず、それだけで、純文学よりは下位に属するそれ自体で特別の文学を形成する。文学とは、純文学であれ単純なものであれ、感動的な真実や美を教えるために、言語が芸術的に用いられている作品のみを指す。

純文学の目的とは、感情に訴えることである。特に詩や小説を通して、このことは行われる。

"style"とは感情が表現される特殊な形式、文体のことである。

to literature exactly what character is to the writer. As no two minds feel exactly alike, — so no two style can be exactly the same. Books cannot make a man's character. Neither can they teach him style. If he wishes to have a style, he must simply try to express his own feeling as truthfully and as clearly as he possibly can.

The difference between literature proper, and other work, — such as philosophy or history, is that literature touches the emotions, not merely the intellect. The effect of literature is in the direction of pleasure and pain, love and hatred, hope and fear.

The difficulty in comprehending foreign literature is not linguistic, or grammatical, but physiological.

to literature exactly what character is to the writer. As no two minds feel exactly alike, — so no two styls* can be exactly the same. Books cannot ~~be~~ ^make a man's character. Neither can they teach him style. If he wishes to have a style, he must quickly try to express his own feelings as truthfully and as clearly as he possibly can.

    The difference between literature proper, and other work, — such as philosophy or history, is that literature touches the <u>emotions</u>, not merely the intellect. The effect of literature is in the direction of pleasure and pain, love and hatred, hope and fear.

    The difficulty in comprehending foreign literature is not linguistic, or grammatical, but physiological.

---

* styles

文学における文体とは、作者における性格と同じである。二つの心が全く同じということはないように二つの文体が全く同じであることはありえない。本は人の性格を形成することはできないし、文体を教えることもできない。もし自分の文体を持ちたいと思うなら、すみやかに、自分自身の感情をできるだけ正直にはっきりと表現しようとつとめるべきだ。

　文学そのものとそのほかの言語作品、哲学や歴史などとの違いは文学は人の知性を刺激するだけでなく、感情、すなわち心の琴線に触れることである。文学の効果とは、喜びや苦しみ、愛や憎しみ、希望や恐れという方向にある。

　外国文学を理解することのむずかしさは言語的や文法的なものではなく、生理的なものにある。

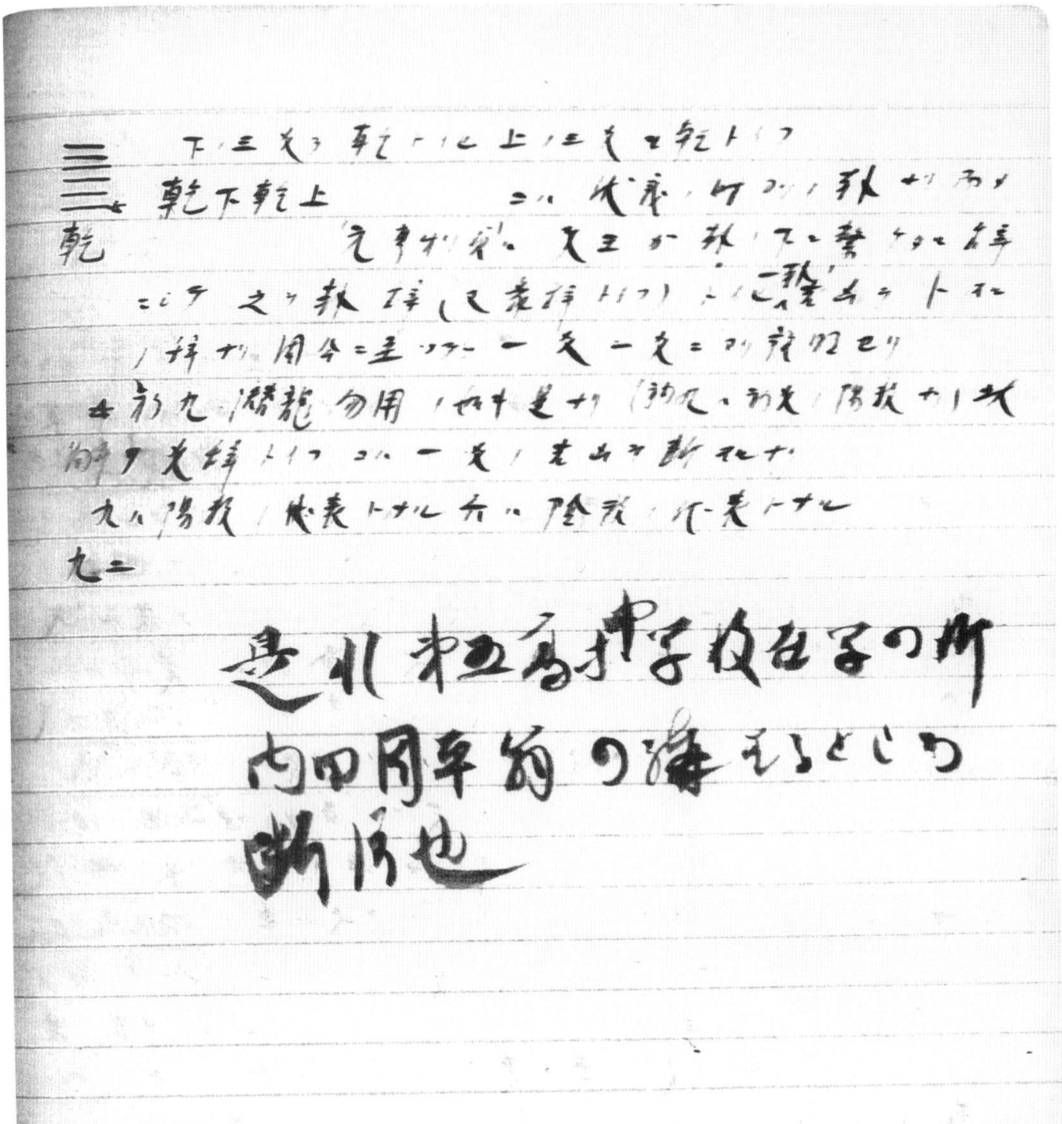

下ノ三爻ヲ乾ト云ヒ上ノ三爻モ乾トイフ
乾下乾上　コハ伏羲ノ作ラレシ卦ナルヲ
乾
元亨利貞ハ文王ガ卦ノ下ニ繋ケル辞
ニシテ之ヲ彖辞（又卦辞トイフ）ト云フ
ノ辞ナリ周公ニ至リテ一爻一爻ニツキ説明セリ
初九　潜龍勿用　ノ如キ是ナリ（初九ハ初爻ノ陽爻ナリ）此ノ辞ヲ爻辞トイフ　コハ一爻ノ意ヲ断ズルナリ
九ハ陽爻ノ代表トナル六ハ陰爻ノ代表トナル
九二
是は東亜高等学校在学の折
内田周平翁の講をまとめし
断片也

内田周平の講義ノートについて

平川祐弘

　このノートにはなお末尾に漢学の、それも易学についての講義が最終頁から始まって八頁書き留められている。黒板は墨で「是れ第五高等中学校在学の折内田周平翁の講ずるところの断片也」と書いている。

　内田周平（一八五七―一九四四）とは何者か。「遠湖内田周平先生は、蔚然たる当今の儒宗であり、道学の棟梁であり、今日東洋思想、儒学、道学方面に志をもつ人々なら何人とて先生の名を知らぬ人はない」と柳田泉は尾佐竹猛編著『明治文化の新研究』（一九四四）で書いた。そしてまた「然るに遠湖先生には又独逸文学者として今一つの面があり、明治二十年前後の文學界に少からざる啓蒙的寄与をされてゐる」。徳富蘇峰は昭和八年遠湖老人の喜寿の筵で、内田周平を単に山崎闇斎の学統を継ぐ学者としてだけではなく、次のような人でもあったとその三十代初めの『国民之友』誌上での文筆活動を紹介した。

　「独逸学を御やりになつて、さうして漢学が出来る。詰り両刀使であるといふやうな事で、其の時分に漢学をやる人は、どうも横文字を知らず、横文字を知つて居る者は余り漢学の方は巧くない。其の両方をやるやうな人は、仏蘭西学の方では中江兆民先生が居られた。……独逸学の方では実に此処におゐでの内田先生でありまして……」

　その内田周平は竹山道雄の母逸の姉継の夫である。竹山は一九五三年、随筆『最後の儒者』でこの伯父が若いころドイツ文学者として活躍したとはまったく知らなかったとして、伯父の家庭についてまことに印象深い一文を書いた。私も『竹山道雄と昭和の時代』（藤原書店、二〇一三年）で竹山の母方の人びとの大切な一人として詳しくふれた。たとえ留学せずとも、同時代人で坪内逍遥にはシェイクスピア、森田思軒にはヴェルヌという個性が刻印された翻訳がある。そうした人に比べて内田には個人の名を冠するような訳業がなかった。それに加えて、蘇峰は喜寿の筵ではふれなかったが、『国民之友』から内田周平を追い落とす恐るべき実力者がドイツから帰ってきた。森鷗外である。鷗外は内田よりも五歳若いが東大医学部では逆に内田より四学年年上で、一八八八（明治二十一）年九月にドイツから帰国するや、翌明治二十二年夏『国民之友』五十八号に訳詩『於母影』を発表する。そして同年十月発行の『柵草紙』で『国民之友』五十九及び六十一号に出た内田訳シラーの『菩提樹畔の逍遥』をつぶさに、徹底的に批評した。鷗外の指摘は正鵠を射ていた。自分の非力を思い知らされたからであろうか、内田はドイツ文学紹介の仕事から身を引いた。そして明治二十五年、熊本の第五高等学校へ漢学の教師として赴任した。ハーンは前年の十一月に熊本に赴任していた。熊本には内田の東京時代の師の一人だった漢学者秋月悌次郎がいて、明治二十六年、秋月の古稀に際して刊行された『鎮西余響』には内田周平

が五高関係者に乞われて序をつけ、ハーンもまた敬愛する秋月翁のために祝辞を寄せている。しかし内田がハーンと交際した形跡はない。内田は東大の学生時代にもドイツ人教師と親しくつきあった形跡のない人である。内田周平講義ノートの内容を云々する力は私にはなく、ハーンとは関係がないので覆刻しなかったが、念のため書き添える。

黒板勝美ノートの裏表紙の裏面。右下に「ENGLISH COMPOSI-TION」「くろいたかつみ」の文字がみえる。

《解説》黒板勝美の生涯

關田かをる

　黒板勝美は、明治七（1874）年九月三日、長崎県東波杵郡下波佐見村田ノ頭郷の旧大村藩士黒板要平の長男として生まれた（『黒板勝美先生遺文』吉川弘文館、1974年、以下、履歴事項は同書による）。

　明治二十三（1890）年、長崎県大村尋常中学校を卒業し、熊本の第五高等中学校へ進学した。翌年十一月二十四日に松江から赴任したラフカディオ・ハーンに、黒板は明治二十五年から二十六年の夏まで英文法や英会話および英文学とラテン語を学んだ。

　ハーンが第五高等中学校の学生から受けた初印象は、松江の尋常中学校の生徒とはたいへん違うものであった。作品「九州の学生とともに」（*Out of the East, 1895*）の冒頭で「学生たちは boys とはまず呼べない」と言い、こう述べている。松江の中学生より年長であるからだけでなく、学生たちは「九州魂」というか「侍気質」がまだ残っており、謹厳で寡黙な大人である。言動や振舞いが人におもねらず率直で、質実剛健を旨とする立ち居振る舞いなので、外見からはとても理解しがたく、松江のような古風で親しみのもてた師弟関係は望めないだろう、と。

　しかし学生たちが書いた英作文は、彼らが情緒面で個性のひらめきをもち、自分で感じたことを率直に表現する姿をみせた。ハーンは作品のなかに彼らの英作文を十二編も取りあげている。ハーンがいかに彼らに魅了され、しだいに日本人の心を奥深く理解していった様子が読み取れよう。

　学生の黒板はハーンに親しみをもつようになり、友人の藤崎八三郎（松江時代からのハーンの教え子）に案内されて、手取本町のハーン居宅をたびたび訪問した。彼の回想に詳しく書かれている。

　明治二十六（1893）年七月、黒板は第五高等中学校を卒業し、九月に帝国大学文科大学の国史科に入学した。在学中の明治二十九年五月、『史學雜誌』に「大日本人名辞書を評す」を、六月にも同誌に「北畠親房事蹟考」（笹川種郎と共著）を発表し、翌七月に大学を卒業した。九月、大学院へ進学するとともに、経済雑誌社に入り、田口卯吉（鼎軒）のもとで『国史大系』の校訂にたずさわる。同年十月十六日、帝国大学史料編纂事項取調補助を嘱託され、明治三十四年四月十五日に同史料編纂員となった。

　明治三十五（1902）年一月三十一日、黒板は東京帝国大学文科大学講師となる。ここで、明治二十九年九月より講師をつとめるハーンの同僚になった。したがって、翌年三月の小泉八雲解雇事件のときには、国史科の教員として黒板は事件の経緯を身近に仄聞していたにちがいない。

明治三十七（1904）年九月二十六日に八雲が没した。同年十一月に刊行された『帝國文学』の「小泉八雲記念号」に、黒板は「熊本時代のヘルン氏」と題した一文を寄稿した。ハーンの授業での具体的な様子ばかりでなく、ハーンが父のように慕った漢学教師の秋月胤久（悌次郎）との親交ぶりも、後に実証史家として台頭する黒板の眼を通して描かれている。
　ところで、私が平成二十五年九月、東京大学文学部英文学研究室所蔵の「市河文庫」でみつけた「英文筆記」には、ノートのはじめの空白ページに墨筆でつぎのように書かれている。

　　　この英文筆記ハ余第五高等中学ニありし比　ラフカヂオ・ヘルン（小泉八雲）氏の口
　　授するところ　今にしてこれを読むも　猶興味津々たるを覚ゆ
　　　　　　　　　　　　大正十二年九月廿有一日夕
　　　　　　　　　　　　　　　　　　　勝美記

　これは、当時東京帝国大学教授で英文学の主任であった市河三喜がラフカディオ・ハーン書簡集を編纂するため、ハーンの教え子たちに呼びかけて収集した資料のひとつであろう。表紙裏には三喜のつぎのような一文も書かれている。

Idiom ニ二種アリ Common idiom, Literary idiom 是ナリ　Literary idiom ハ時トシテ Special meaning ヲ有スルニヨリ好ンテ之ヲ用ヰルコト勿レ Common idiom ハ之ヲ適當ニ用ヰル時ハ　文簡潔大ニ愛ス可キノ文トナル可シ
　　　Spontaneity.[sic]
　<u>一讀スベキモノナリ</u>　　　Ｉ. 生

　なお、「英文筆記」ノートの末尾の裏表紙の裏面には ENGLISH と COMPOSI-TION が組み合わされた横長の印章と「くろいた」の文字の下に「かつみ」が横に刻された縦長の楕円形の大きな印章（3.5cm）の二つが押印されていた。彼の蔵書印ではないだろうか。
　「英文筆記」は 67 ページにわたって書かれている。これはハーンが板書した授業内容を筆記したものであり、回想「熊本時代のヘルン氏」に書かれていた記述の一端を補強するばかりでなく、その後 23 年を経てもなお、彼が「興味津々たるを覚ゆ」と記したほど、ハーンの英語の教え方がいかに学生を魅了するものであったか、それが明らかな興味深い資料である。
　つまり、平成二十五年三月に刊行された『ラフカディオ・ハーンの英語教育　友枝高彦・高田力・中土義敬のノートから』と同じく、黒板による自筆の「英文筆記」もまたハーンの授業風景のみならず、ハーンの英語教育に対する感性が臨場感をもって迫ってくる。

ハーンの教育者としての狭い側面でなく、全体像を再考させる意味でも、貴重な資料であるといわねばならない。

明治三十八（1905）年四月一日、文科大学助教授に任じられ、史料編纂官を兼ねた。同年十一月十八日、「日本古文書様式論」（明治三十六年脱稿）で文学博士の学位を取得したように、以後、古文書を資料とする実際的、実証的な研究に先鞭をつけた。古来からの基本文献を収集した『国史大系』を編修校訂し、刊行したことは、黒板の名を日本史学界における不朽のものとした。

明治三十九（1906）年十月に、浅田栄次、安孫子貞治郎との共編で『エスペラント日本辞書』を刊行している。

明治四十一（1908）年二月、学術研究のため私費でヨーロッパにでかけ、七月にロンドンの国際平和主義大会、八月にはベルリンの国際歴史学会議にも参加した。しかも、ドレスデンで開催された万国エスペラント大会に出席しているところに、黒板の国際性をみる想いがする。二年間にわたる旅で、黒板は欧米における史学研究と遺蹟・遺物の保存に関して豊富な知識を得て、明治四十三年に帰国した。

大正四（1915）年九月、国史学第二講座を担当する。

大正八（1919）年七月、史料編纂官兼東京帝国大学教授に就任し、史料編纂掛事務主任をつとめた。翌年に史料編纂官を退任して、東京帝国大学教授専任となり、官学アカデミズムにおける日本史学研究の最高権威者に位置づけられる。古文書学の体系を樹立し、実証主義的な日本史学研究の基礎を確立した功績は大きかった。

門下生に相田二郎、坂本太郎、羽仁五郎、平泉澄（ひらいずみきよし）、丸山二郎ら（五十音順）がいる。小泉家の縁者で、八雲のアシスタントであった三成重敬（みなりしげゆき）は、明治三十一年に従兄弟で、当時東京帝国大学法科大学長の梅謙次郎の紹介で東京大学の史料編纂掛写字生として入所して、三上参次や黒板勝美らの助手をつとめ、昭和二十九年まで史料編纂所に勤務した。およそ半世紀の永きにわたり黒板とともに、『大日本古文書』の編纂、東寺百合文書、東山御文庫や醍醐寺文書の史料調査に従事した人物である。

黒板は専門の『国史大系』編纂事業のほか、国宝の調査、文化財の保存事業に尽力した。昭和九（1934）年には独力で日本古文化研究所を創設して所長となり、藤原宮跡の調査を実地に発掘し史実を確定した。法隆寺国宝保存会や、日光、高野山、醍醐寺、鎌倉等の宝物館設立など、多方面に活躍している。

社会的関心も高かった。明治期には平民社に出入りし、昭和八年に治安維持法違反の容疑で検挙された羽仁五郎の釈放に尽力した。

このように、黒板勝美は専門分野における日本史学の基礎的な文献刊行事業や文化財の保存事業に帝大教授として先頭に立って取り組んだ。その一方で、海外調査に積極的に出かけ、外国での良き事例を参考にして、多くを吸収した。昭和二（1927）年から翌年にかけての海外調査でも、出張とはいえ、東西ヨーロッパの歴史学者たちと交流を図った。国

際奨学金制度を創設したアルベール・カーンの資金で出張したので、パリに着くや彼と会い、親交を深めた。ベルリンでは帝国大学で史学を学んだ恩師ルードヴィッヒ・リース博士を訪ね、さらにイギリスではデヴォンシアのセント・メアリーに隠棲するサー・アーネスト・サトウを訪問した。当時の日記にはこうした外国人との交流の日々が綴られている。

　昭和十（1935）年、定年により退官して、東京帝国大学名誉教授となる。翌年、旅行途上の高崎市で脳溢血のため倒れ、療養十年後の昭和二十一年十二月二十一日に渋谷の自宅で死去（享年七十三）、池上本門寺に葬られた（法名は文耕院虚心日勝大居士）。

（日本比較文学会会員）

熊本時代のヘルン氏

黒板勝美

　此ヘルン君の事を誰でも能くハーンと言ふやうですが、我々が熊本に来られた時に聞きました名前は矢張りヘルンと聞いて居つた、熊本の高等学校で出版になりました報告などの中にも矢張りラフカヂオヘルンと書いてあつた、併し綴りから言つたらば矢張ハーンの方が宜いやうに思ふ。

　熊本には出雲の方から来られたやうに覚えて居りますが、来られた初には別に有名な文学者とか何とかいふやうな考はなくて、唯有り来りの外国教師、イングリッシュの教師と我々は思ふて居つた。併し段々レクチュアの仕方でありますとか、其外我々に質問される有様から考へて見て、段々今までの経歴を聞いて見ますといふと、既に亜米利加に居らるゝ頃からして多少名が著はれた方であるといふことを知つたので、それから一般の注意に上つて来たやうである。一番初め来られた時の先生に対する考は、非常に変な方で、極く明瞭にレクチュアをされるので、今まで居られた外国教師の非常に難解な聞き悪いレクチュアに比して我々は非常に好意を以て迎へた。けれどもまだ文学の趣味であるとかいふ方の側までには我々の学問が進歩して居なかつた時代ですから、唯それだけの感じを以て先生を迎へて居つた。併し先生が来られましてから段々レトリックであるとか、コンバーセーションであるとかいふやうなものを習つた結果は、非常に我々の間に文学的趣味を注入されたやうに思ふ。一番しまいにはラテン語と英文学の二つを受持つて居られたが、英文学史のレクチュアで一番趣味を感じたのは、シエクスピーアの講義に付て、今まで、シエクスピーアといふことは唯名前は皆言ふのですが、どんな風な傾向を持て、どんな風な詩人で有つたといふことは始めて知つたので、それまではキングリヤなどいふことは口には言ふけれども、実際どういふ意味を以て書いたとか、どういふ風にシエクスピーアの天才を現はして居るとかいふやうなことは分らずに居つて、僅にミーニングでも知つて居れば宜いが、それさへも覚束ない位であつた。其講義は一週間二時間位で、チョーサから始められてジョージエリオットまでゞ済んで仕舞つたと思ふ。其シエクスピーアの講義の終つたのが二学期であつたが、其時終ひの文句に「シエクスピーアの講義が終つて、さうして二学期の終りのベルが鳴つた」といふやうなことを言つた、それは余程面白い洒落た文句であつたと思ふ。其時分は黒板に大体を書きまして、其後で又詳しく自分で話をするといふ訳であつた。ですから筆記する方は楽であつた、それで能く分る言葉ですから殆ど分らないといふことは義理にも言へない訳であつた、それだから皆喜んで居つた。実に易［わかりやす］い言葉で、詰り程度で言つたらば第三リーダーか第四リーダー位の言葉であつた。外の人との折合は極く宜い方であつて、殊に秋月胤久［あきづきかづひき］といふ漢学の教師があつたが、其人は会津で非常に働いた人であつて、其時は七十歳ばかりで、髯が真白に生へて、如何にも

愉快な顔をして子供でも懐（なつ）くといふやうな人であつたが、ヘルン君は自ら其人を神だと言つて居つた。さうして両人逢ひますと、秋月君は平気で「今日は」「お早う」といふやうなことを言ふ、所がヘルン君は其時分日本語をチッとも知らぬから、妙な顔をして礼をする、秋月君が搆はず話して居ると向ふは黙つて聞いて居るといふ風、これはフロムゼイースト［From the East］の中に書いてあつたやうである。始終往復されて居つたやうである。此秋月君は四五年前故人に為られましたが、序（ついで）に此人の御話をしますと、倫理学を受持つて居られましたが、皆を集めて話をして居ると直ぐ政治上の問題になつて来る、学問をするのは廟堂の上に立つて天下を料理する為めである、大工や左官になるのが学問をする目的でないといふやうなことを言つて法科をやるのは弁護士か裁判官になるとしか思はない、文学が一番受けが宜い、即ち古い考で、昌平黌に這入つて居つて政治をやつたといふやうな考の人であつた。其時藤崎といふ人が熊本に居られた、軍人であつて、其人の妻君といふのがヘルン君の妻君の極く近い親類か何かの関係になつて居る、それで其養子といふ者がヘルン君の家に預けてあつた、さういふ関係で丁度熊本にヘルン君が来られてから能く往復して居つた、其藤崎といふ人と私と懇意であつたからヘルン君の家にも遊びに行くやうになつた。幾度も行つたが、或時行きました時の記憶に依ると、冬であつたと思ひますが、和服を着し、例の如く煙管を五六本傍に持つて来て、詰め換へては飲んで、さうして色々話をする、こちらは別に聞くことはないが、亜米利加あたりの話をし、昔仏蘭西領のルイヂニヤに行かれた時に、熊本も暖かい所で蚊が多いがルイヂニヤの蚊は此処のよりも余程大きいなどゝいふ話をして居つた、それから日本の庭は好きだが、西洋のは幾何学的でいかない、どうも風味がないなどゝ言つて居られた。日本語は教場などでも少しも遣（つか）はない。

　作文の題は自分の遭遇したこと又は感じたことなどを一週間又は二週間の間に書いて来いとか、又は昔話を書いて来いとかいふやうなことであつた。

　其時分余り外に出たやうなことはなかつた、人々との交際も余りなかつたやうです、併し東京に来られた時よりも人に会はれたやうです。

　生徒の頭に一番感じたのは、其以前の教師が牧師見たやうな人であつたのに、それと反対に非常に基督教嫌ひであるといふことであつたやうです。今まで外国教師の為めに造つてある校舎にも、這入らず、別に家を一軒借りて居られた、それから其家の附近に教会堂があるからいやだといふので外に引越された。

　外にイングリッシュを教へて居つたのは佐久間信恭といふ人でした、それから教頭が今彼処の校長であるが桜井房記といふ人で、此人は仏蘭西語の出身であるから先生とは仏蘭西語で話をして居られた。

　我々が一緒に写真を撮るやうな時は来て其中に加はる位で、いつでも半面の写真を撮られた、質問などには能く答へられた、会などには余り見掛けんやうにおぼえます、或は御呼び申さなかつた方が多いかも知れぬ。

其時分の私の同窓で大学に参つた者は、二十九年の卒業生で、法科の安住、古森、是は二人とも地方裁判所に居ります、それから今山口県の書記官になつて居る林一蔵といふ人などです。

　ヘルン君は熊本時代に於てはそんなに快活だといふことは言へませぬが、人嫌ひといふやうな傾向は見えなかつたやうに感ずる。私は東京で一度訪問しました、三十年か三十一年でした、其時は洋服でした、御閑ですかと言つたら、ちつとも閑は持たないと言つて居られた、多分何にか書いておられた時の様でした。熊本で教授の時分にも草稿などはなかつたやうに感じます、尤も草稿を作る程むづかしいものではなかつたでせう。教授受持の時間は我々のが一週三時間、其下が二時間位、皆で十時間か十二時間位であつたと思ひます。

　家は普通の日本家で、元あつた大きな家を買ひまして、庭などの大変広い何とかいふ神社の半町か一町ばかり先であつた、初の家は前言ふ通り基督教の鐘の音がいやだといふので引越されたといふことであつた。是は藤崎君の話であつたが、歩く時でも教会堂のある所は避けて行くといふ風であつたさうです、其家から学校までは十町位もあつたでせう。英語か仏語の出来る者とは話が出来た、秋月君などが家に行かれると妻君が通弁をしたのであらうと思ふ。其時分は子供さんがまだ出来ないと思ふ、それ故家族は極く少なかつた。私がヘルンさんを知つて居るのは二十五年から六年の夏までゞす。私が能く訪ねて行つた部屋は十二畳位のもので、床の間の飾などは日本流であつた、床の間の直ぐ側に座つて話をされる、障子を開けると直ぐ庭が見える、さうして始終坐つて居られた、たんぜん見たやうな羽織を着て居つたやうに思ふ。学校にはいつも洋服ばかり着て来られる、其時の風采はこちらに来られても変はらぬやうに思ふ、極く質素の服装で、灰色の洋服で、帽子は茶であつた。学校は休まれたことがなく、非常に勉強な人でした。

　羅甸語〔ラテン〕は其時分学科の正科であつた。其時代には文科では天文までやつた。本科になつてからケミストリーなどもやり、物理もやつた、其時分は一般の高等学校がさうであつたと思ふ。外のテクストリーヂングは重もにコンバーセーションといふ方でしたからあるまいと思ふ、コンバーセーションは直〔すぐ〕にていねいに直して下すつた。此コンバーセーションの時に面白いことがある、何でも宜いから思つたことを言へといふやうな主義であつたので、既に故人となつた神川といふ人でしたが、「足懸け三年」といふことを言つた、其「足懸」といふことは向ふの言葉にないので、日本語の直訳流にフートハンギング、スリイヤースとやつた、それがどうしても先生に分らぬ、そこでフートハンギングの説明をやつたので、是は面白いと言つて自分で書いて行かれたことがある。

　先生の来られた初に今までの外国教師と違つて非常に分り宜いやうに話をされた一例として御話しますと、ラーヂといふ字とビッグといふ字の遣ひ分の場合でもちやんと図に書いて、ラーヂといふ方は長方形のやうなものである、大きいといふけれども唯長さが大きくて、そんなに奥行は深くない、それからビッグといふと長くして奥行も深い、其方が力

がある字である、脊の大きい者をラーヂといふけれども肥つたといふ方はビッグでなければならぬといふ風に、それを図に書いて教へらるるから我々の頭には其後ビッグとラーヂの遣ひ分に付て迷ふといふやうなことはない。それからもう一つ一番初めに私の感じたのはオッフンといふ言葉をオフツンと発音したこと、ハンブルをアンブルと発音されたことなどである。それからラテンの教授法はラテンコースをやつて、自分でエキサーサイズをさして順番に聴く、それで大変面白いことがある、大概首（はじ）めに居る人からズットやるが、それを時々反対にやる、調べて居る人は宜いけれども、調べない人は自分は何番だといふので其処だけ調べて居る、それが反対に来ると折々恐慌を来たした。採点などは極く宜い方で、私などは九十五六点以下を貰つたことはない、外にリッデルといふ教師が居つたが、それは宣教師であつたが、それとは交際がなかつた、僕等は基督教を研究しやうといふのでなく、イングリッシュを一週間に二回稽古に行つたが、其報酬として日曜日にバイブルを聴きに行つた、本田増次郎君が其人の飜訳をして居つたが、時々僕等にやらせられて下手な飜訳をしたことがある。

　ヘルン君は斯ういふことを言つて居られた、出雲に行つたのは出雲が日本の一番古国である、神代といふものは出雲に在るといふ話を聞いて招きに応じたのであると言つて居られたが、我々はヘルン君が基督嫌ひで神道が良いと言つて居るのは不思議だといふ感じを持つて居りました。

　会話は先生が問ひを懸け、学生の方も亦問ひを懸けて話をする、話の中に言葉が悪いと、斯ういふ風に言はなければならぬと言つて直して呉れられた。コンポジションの方は学生が家から作つて行くと、それを直して面白いものに付て批評をする、又それに付て自分の話をするといふやうなことであつた。

　英文学史のは重もにチョーサから始めて、其時代は余程詳しかつた、それからシエクスピアが殆ど一学期であつた、それからテニソンの話もあつたやうに思ふ、ジョージエリオットまで行かない中にテニソンの話があつたやうに思ふ、唯エリオットのことを大層えらい人のやうに先生が言つたからそれで覚えて居る、ミルトンは極めてザットであつた、バンヤンの話も極く簡略であつた、ジョンソンの話とスキフトは大分詳しかつた、私はジョージエリオット本名がエバンスといふことなども其時始めて知つた、ジョージといふから男だと思つて居ると、女であるといふから、どういふ訳かと質問したことなどを覚えて居る。

　日本の昔話に付ては余程インテレストを感じて居つたやうに思ふ、詰り桃太郎の話などであるが、私などがそれを書くには必ず初めにワンス、アポン、エタイムといふことが附く。レトリックの講義の仕方は重もに字の置工合と、ミーターやクライマックスになつて行く具合なぞで、詰まるところ、先生の分り易い言葉といふものが多少我々の記憶に遺つて居る所以で、若しむづかしくやられると何を言つたのだか分らなかつたと思ふ。

　東京に来られた初に牛込富久町に居られたが、其直ぐ近所に瘤寺といふ寺がある。其境

内が非常に好きで毎日散歩に行かれた、丁度其処に大きな杉の木がある、それが大変気に入つて、大概其処を見廻る、自身の家からも其杉の木が見えるやうになつて居つたが、其瘤寺の坊さんが必要があつたか何かで其杉の木を伐つて仕舞つた、それを非常に残念に思はれて頻に坊さんに苦情を言ひに行つたが、自分の片腕を切られたやうに思ふと言つて落胆して、竟[つい]に家まで引越されたといふことである。一体先生は植木が好きで、今の家にも愛された植木がたくさんあるといふことを聞いて居ります。

（『帝國文學』第十巻十一号、一九〇四年十一月）

五高に於けるヘルン先生

白壁傑次郎

　私は明治二十四年から二十七年まで五高に在學致しました。ヘルン先生も丁度此三ケ年間五高に勤務されたのです。それで熊本に於ける先生の事に就ては一番能く知つて居るべき筈の一人であります。成程先生の教授振りに就ては能く存じて居ます、中々親切なものでノート一片持たれるではないが前置詞の講義をされる時など今でも能く覺えて居ます。其語の含む意義を能く御話されて後は全部實例で凡て黑板に記されました。其れが實に豊富で自由自在で生徒が質問することあれば直ぐ實例を示される。眞に心地よき活々した教授振りでありました。科學的の教授法に適つて居たかは存じませんが心地よく愉快であつた事は事實です。私と一諸に五高に在學した人々で今熊本に居られるのは法學士赤星典太古閑又五郎農學士木下彌八郎理學士高山虎太の諸氏です。此等の方々に特にヘルン先生の事に就て御記憶の事もあらばと存じ御訪ね致して見ましたが先生の御家庭に訪問された様の事もなく先生の日常に就て特に御存じと申す事はありませんでした。先生の日常に就ては先生自から記された委しき御手簡が小泉八雲と言ふ著書に譯載されて居ます。此書籍は高山虎太氏の御紹介で先生の松江中學時代に於ける生徒の今は熊本に暮されて居る先生とは最も御懇意なりし一人の陸軍大佐藤崎八三郎氏から拜借しました。此手簡の一部を載せたら何ふかと井上君に相談致して置きました。藤崎氏から種々の事を承はりましたが熊本に於ける先生には關係が少ないですから止めます。先生の御勤勉であつた事と御親切であつた事は種々の方面から窺はれます。次の様な事に思ひ至れば一種の感に打たれます。先生は五高に於ては一週實に二十七時間の受持ちがあつたと言ふ事です。それにラテン語や時にはフランス語も受持たれたとの事。此種々の學科を受持つと言ふ事が教師には中々の痛手です。それだのに生徒の出した英作文は時を違へず丁寧に訂し親切に評を加へて返されました。尙其當時は知りませんでしたが後から聞きますれば熊本の三年間に三冊もの著書の批判を世界に問はれた相です、教場での教授ではノートこそ御用ひになりませんでしたが彼の整然振りから考へれば必ずノートを作るに劣らぬ苦心の準備があつたと思はれます。私は大學でダイヴァースと言ふ英國人の先生に無機化學を教はりました。先生の受持ちは無機化學一週三時間夫れに一學期間であつたが生理化學の講義が一週三時間計六時間でありました。ノートは全然持たれません。成程夏冬の區別なく朝八時から午后四時迄は一日の休みなく研究され又學生の研究に對し指導されました。普通は一週三時間の講義です。それだのに講義の用意をするに中々骨が折れる時間が不足勝ちだと申された事を耳にして居ます。眞の學者の心掛けは又別だと私は感心しました。又曾つて五高の教授であつて今は山高の教頭である英語教授の戶澤氏と語つたときに氏の言に笑つて「英語に上手下手はない評判がよいとか何とか言ふのは其先生が如何程勉強して居るか丈の差です」との

事でした。可なり餘分の事を申しましたが五高に於けるヘルン先生の事など思ひ浮べて見ると今更ら同情に堪へません。うんと鍛へ上ぐれば別だと言ふ談もないではありませんが兎に角用意不充分で教場に出る時は輕微の頭痛位は必ずするものです。ヘルン先生の教授には私等は充分の滿足を感じて居た。然しヘルン先生の御心中は如何なりしか二十七時もの授業に對して心行く準備の出來る筈なく或は多く不充分に感じて居られたかと推察される。又生命たる著述の時間は殆んどなし、寧ろ心苦しき氣味で居られたかと察せられます。恐らく其爲でしやう三年の契約期限が終りに近くと五高外二、三の學校からも交渉があつたに拘はらず二百圓の俸給をすてて幾分か暇の得易き神戸クロニクル新聞社に百圓で赴任されました。其頃クロニクルには私の友人の有馬と申す男が居ました。明治二十八年の事でしたかハーンの談を頻りに試み氏は偉がられて居ると言つてました。日淸戰爭の時だから氏のペンも揮はれた事でしやう。此ハーン氏が五高のヘルン先生の事です。ヘルン先生が五高に居られた時先生の長男が誕生されました。先生の御喜びは一通でなく朝夕柄の附いた大きな蟲眼鏡を手にして之を眺めて居られると言ふ事が生徒の間に傳はりました。先生は此兒を神として尊ばれて居ると言ふ事でした。先生は片眼で著るしく飛び出て居ました。非常な近視眼で並の近視鏡では用をなさぬ。それで右様のレンズを持つて居られました。此レンズなき時は殆んど盲目と等しく黑板に書かれるのにも見て書かれるのでなく手と心で書かれたのです。此種のレンズを用ひた人は私の知つて居る範圍内では文部次官辻氏と先生との二人限りです。前申しました様に先生に長男が御生れになつたので私等數人連れで一度先生の御家庭を訪問致しました。誕生の御祝を申上る爲めに。其時の連れが誰々であつたか今覺えて居ません。其時種々な御話を承はりました。先づ先生は最も御氣入りだと言はれて居る橋形に柄の附いた古風の煙草盆を提げて出て來られました。そして座蒲團に奇麗に座られ挨拶をして近傍に刀掛けの様な臺に掛けてあつたと覺えてますが幾本かの長い煙管の内一本を靜かに取つて幾分か來歷の説明を加へて煙草を喫はれました。それから生徒からの種々の挨拶や問に對する先生の御言葉ですが英語の事ですから身に著いた様に分りも致しませず又覺えても居ません然し何回でも問ひ返すのですから先生の意は大略腑に落ちた様でした。其時バツドイングリシとブロークンイングリシとの區別なども覺えた様でした。誰か一人が吾々の様なブロークンイングリシでと申しましたら先生がブロークンではない其意ならばバツドと言ふべきだ。ブロークンとは上海あたりで用ひて居るもので立派に定つた一つのイングリシになつて居る然し本當のイングリシではないと言はれた様です。先生の此程御誕生の御兒様や奥様に對せらるる考は丁度神にでも對せらるるかの如きものであつた様です。此れは私の感ですが誰でも人生を考ふる程の人に取つては現實界に於て妻や兒程不可思議のものはあまり有りますまい。昨日まで一人で居たものが今日は妻なるものに傳つかれる。束の間に神身共に倍加又は以上になる。夢の如く過す内にやがて兒が神の意を傳へ全身の力を擧げて初めて神意を歌ふ此歌の意味は容易に明亮ならずとも誰か妙の感を起さぬものがありませうか。斯様の感は其時も今も私には變り

ありません。談は移つて誰やらが先生の著述の事に關して一寸御尋ねしました。先生は大變喜ばれて次の様な事を言はれました。此迄あまり反響がなかつた所が此頃種々の有力な評論壇に追々批評が載る様になつて芽を出し初めたと言ふ様の事でした。それから文章や著述に關する様な談になり私の今日でも稍明瞭に覺えて居る先生の御言葉は次の様のものでした。文章が相當自由に書ける様になるには二十年の努力を要する。文章を書くには推敲に推敲を要する。始め十語で表はし得た思想ならば九語か八語か尙少數の語で同じ思想を表はす様に骨折らねばならぬ。六文字綴りの語を用ひて居るならば五文字綴りか四文字綴りで置換へ得る語はないかと探さねばならぬ。ノツトウイヅスタンデイングと言ふ様な恐ろしい語は出來得るならば終生用ひぬがよい。長綴りの語を用ふれば章句の締りが弛む。章句は出來る丈け短かくせねばならぬと言ふ様の事でした。實例を擧げてマコーレイだつたか其極く若い時にヘスチングであつたかを書きたくつて後年大に悔いたと言ふ様な事を言はれました。又一つ加へられたのは母語でない語葉で文學的の著述をなすのは稍愚に近い、如何に努めても多數の讀者の心の琴線に觸れる事は困難であると言ふ意でした。談の間に先生は例の柄付の眼鏡で挨拶の爲め客間に抱かれた御長男を能く視られました。私達は喜々として左様ならを申しました。回顧すれば三十三ケ年前の或る温かき夕でした。

　　　　　　　　　　　　　　　　　　　　（茫然とした記錄を辿つて）

〈編著者略歴〉

平川祐弘（ひらかわ・すけひろ）

　1931年東京に生まれる。1953年東京大学教養学部教養学科卒業。仏伊給費留学生。1964年東大大学院比較文学比較文化課程担当助手。1992年東大定年退官、名誉教授。
　著書、『和魂洋才の系譜』（博士論文、河出書房新社、平凡社ライブラリー）、『西欧の衝撃と日本』（講談社、絶版）、『マッテオ・リッチ伝』（平凡社東洋文庫）、『天ハ自ラ助クルモノヲ助ク──中村正直と『西国立志編』』（名古屋大学出版会）、『アーサー・ウェイリー『源氏物語』の翻訳者』（白水社）、『ダンテ『神曲』講義』（河出書房新社）、『書物の声　歴史の声』（弦書房）、『竹山道雄と昭和の時代』（藤原書店）他。
　ハーン関係は次の通り。『小泉八雲──西洋脱出の夢』(1981, サントリー学芸賞)、『破られた友情──ハーンとチェンバレンの日本理解』(1987)、『小泉八雲とカミガミの世界』(1988)、『オリエンタルな夢──小泉八雲と霊の世界』(1996)、『ラフカディオ・ハーン──植民地化・キリスト教化・文明開化』(2004, ミネルヴァ書房、和辻賞)、編著 *Rediscovering Lafcadio Hearn* (Global Oriental, 1997)、*Lafcadio Hearn in International Perspectives* (Global Oriental, 2006)、*A la recherche de l'identité japonaise—le shintō interprété par les écrivains européens* (L'Harmattan, 2012)、『小泉八雲事典』(2000)、『講座小泉八雲』(2009, 新曜社)、編訳『小泉八雲名作選集』六巻（講談社学術文庫）、翻訳 小泉八雲『骨董・怪談』（河出書房新社, 2014）

ラフカディオ・ハーンの英語クラス
Lafcadio Hearn's English Class
──黒板勝美のノートから

2014年10月25日発行

編　者　　平川祐弘Ⓒ

発行者　　小野静男

発行所　　弦書房

　　　　　〒810-0041　福岡市中央区大名2-2-43ELKビル301
　　　　　TEL 092-726-9885　FAX 092-726-9886
　　　　　E-mail:books@genshobo.com
　　　　　http://genshobo.com/

印　刷　　アロー印刷株式会社
製　本　　株式会社渋谷文泉閣

Ⓒ 2014
落丁・乱丁本はお取替えいたします
ISBN978-4-86329-106-5 C0021

◆教育者としてのハーンを明らかにする一級資料◆

ラフカディオ・ハーンの英作文教育

アラン・ローゼン／西川盛雄

松江時代（明治23〜24年）のラフカディオ・ハーンによる英作文授業のノートを発見、復刻。ハーン直筆の添削跡とコメントが残る、一級資料。資料の分析解説付。　　　　　　　【2刷】3200円＋税

◆ハーンは熊本五高生たちに英語をどのように教えていたのか◆

ラフカディオ・ハーンの英語教育

《友枝高彦・高田力・中土義敬のノートから》

平川祐弘／富山大学附属図書館ヘルン文庫［監修］

明治26〜27年、ハーンから直接英語を習い、授業内容を克明に記録した五高生の《講義ノート》が発見された。この貴重なノートから明らかになるハーンの熊本時代の実像。　　　【2刷】3200円＋税